L.D. HARKRADER

NOCTURNE

L.D. HARKRADER

NOCTURNE

BOOKS FOR
YOUNG READERS

Nocturne

©2010 Wizards of the Coast LLC

Published by Wizards of the Coast LLC

DUNGEONS & DRAGONS, WIZARDS OF THE COAST, and their respective logos are trademarks of Wizards of the Coast LLC in the U.S.A. and other countries.

Printed in the U.S.A.

Cover art by Juliana Kolesova
First Printing: June 2010

9 8 7 6 5 4 3 2 1

ISBN: 978-0-7869-5502-2
ISBN: 978-0-7869-5759-0 (e-book)
620-25397000-001-EN

Library of Congress Cataloging-in-Publication Data

Harkrader, Lisa.
  Nocturne / L.D. Harkrader.
     p. cm.
  Summary: Eager to practice her magic skills but confined to working in her uncle's book shop, teenaged Flan embarks on an adventure with an attractive vampire hunter and discovers startling secrets along the way.
  ISBN 978-0-7869-5502-2
  [1. Magic--Fiction. 2. Vampires--Fiction. 3. Identity--Fiction. 4.Adventure and adventurers--Fiction.] I. Title.
  PZ7.H22615No 2010
  [Fic]--dc22

                                                                                    2009054055

U.S., CANADA,
ASIA, PACIFIC, & LATIN AMERICA
Wizards of the Coast LLC
P.O. Box 707
Renton, WA 98057-0707
+1-800-324-6496

EUROPEAN HEADQUARTERS
Hasbro UK Ltd
Caswell Way
Newport, Gwent NP9 0YH
GREAT BRITAIN
Please keep this address for your records.

Visit our Web site at **DungeonsandDragons.com**

10 11 12 13 14 15 16   WC-FF

To my editor, Nina Hess.
Thank you for your patience, your encouragement,
and your keen vision for story, character, and pacing.
I'm in your debt.

Prologue

Monsieur Anatole stopped, teacup halfway to his lips. He sat very still, listening. Yes, he'd been right. It was nearly midnight on this black and moonless eve, and he'd heard carriage wheels clattering down Wicker Street.

Which, in Monsieur Anatole's experience, was not unusual. The wheels rolled to a halt in the cobblestone street below. Which, in Monsieur Anatole's experience, was not out of the ordinary.

Anatole left his tea and his plate of ginger cookies sitting on the table beside his hearthside chair, pulled his bed jacket close around him, and snatched up his lamp. He left the warmth of the fireplace behind and made his way down the creaking back staircase, running a hand over his wisps of white hair, preparing to answer the knock he knew would soon come.

But before he could make it to the shop below, the wheels abruptly clattered away.

Which, in Monsieur Anatole's experience, was highly odd indeed.

Anatole waited, but no knock sounded on the bookshop door. He sighed, nodded, and turned to make his way back up the stairs. People changed their minds. He had come to expect it.

He did not expect what he heard next—a faint mewling sound, echoing along the narrow street outside his shop.

He waved a hand. "Merely a kitten. Lost in the dark."

Still, he hesitated, not willing to allow even a mere kitten to be swallowed by the dangers of the night.

When the mewl became a cry, Anatole knew the sound came from no kitten.

He picked his way down the stairs and through the maze of overstuffed bookshelves to the front of the shop. He eased the door open, held his lamp high, and peered out into the damp chill of the night. A thick fog cloaked Wicker Street, and at first he saw nothing. But when the creature cried again, nearly at Anatole's feet, he lowered his lamp.

There, in the hollow of the three stone steps that led from the street down to the shop, he found her—a baby girl, bundled in the remnant of a once-fine blanket.

"Well," Anatole smiled down at the crying baby. "This is certainly different from the usual midnight plea for an amulet or shield spell."

Anatole lifted his lamp. He peered through the fog, first one direction, then the other. But no one else was around. The child was alone.

He set his lamp on the step beside the basket and pushed

the blanket from the baby's face. She was a plump child, with rosy skin. She gurgled at the sight of Anatole's face.

"Someone has taken good care of you," Anatole told her.

Tucked in the blanket, he discovered a scrap of rough brown paper, the kind used to wrap parcels. He held it to the lamplight to make out the first line of words:

She will do better with someone of her own kind.

"Someone of her own kind?" Anatole frowned. He pushed the blanket aside and held his lamp so that its light shone over the baby's face. "You look like no one I know, certainly like no one related to me—you're much too lovely. And you could not be a child of mine." He rubbed a knuckle along the bottom of his nose. "I can only think you've been left at the wrong door."

He lifted the lamp to read the remainder of the note:

Magic is a beacon. If it is allowed to shine, evil will find it. Please, sir. Shelter her from that danger. I beg you.

He turned the scrap of paper over. On the other side was a torn bit of writing—*Flannery Lane*. He tucked the scrap back into the basket and stared down at the baby. "Well, now, Flannery Lane. I can't think what could have frightened your family so thoroughly, but if they had known how little this codgy old wizard knows about caring for such a tiny cherub, they'd be more frightened still."

Baby Flannery began to whimper. Anatole peered up and down Wicker Street, and found nothing but a wall of fog.

"I can't leave you here, and I see no one else around, clamoring to care for a baby." He scratched his chin. "I suppose the duty must fall to me." Anatole snuggled the blanket around the baby as best he could and gathered the basket in his arms. "Tomorrow we shall find someone better equipped for the task, but surely even I cannot damage you beyond repair in one short night."

Before pulling the door shut behind him, he peered back out into the night. When still he saw no one, he firmly closed and locked the bookshop door.

As he wound his way toward the stairs, a shadow seemed to fall across the overstuffed shelves and haphazard stacks of books. Anatole's lamp flickered. A chill seeped through the aisles. At once the bookshop seemed blacker than the already deep black of the moonless night.

Anatole turned and, lamp held high, peered through the shop. He thought he caught a movement through the glass.

The baby cried and he shook his head. He hurried upstairs and set the basket in his armchair, beside the warmth of the fire, then turned toward his cupboard.

As he scratched his head, wondering what exactly to feed a creature as foreign to him as the hungry, screaming child, her crying abruptly stopped.

He turned back.

And found baby Flannery clutching a ginger cookie in her chubby pink fist. He looked at the plate of cookies on the table and scratched his head once more. She could not have reached the cookie herself. She was too small, and the table was too high, and she was bundled too tightly in her blanket.

"Ah." Anatole nodded slowly. "The note is suddenly clear."

With a flick of his finger, Anatole levitated a ginger cookie from the table until it hovered in front of him. He grabbed the cookie and took a bite. "'Someone of her own kind.'" He gazed down at the baby and smiled. "Well, little magic-maker, it looks as if we are of a kind. Perhaps we shall make it safely till morning after all."

One
Fifteen years later

Flannery turned the book's thick, yellowed pages. A cloud of timeworn dust wafted up from the spine and she sneezed, rattling the amulets dangling from the peg beside her. She wiped her nose, then held out a hand to still the tinkling gems.

Flan was tending her uncle's shop—Monsieur Anatole's Books, Wonders, and Charms. Although, in truth, she wasn't tending the shop half as diligently as she was tending her own curiosity. She sat hunkered on a high rung of the rolling ladder Uncle Anatole had devised for reaching the tallest of the crowded shelves, feather duster forgotten on a stack of books below. Obsidian lay curled on the shelf beside her, purring. His inky black head rested on his paws, and to all appearances he was fast asleep but for the occasional twitch of a whisker or flick of his tail.

Flan ran her finger down the page as she read, careful not to damage the crumbling edges of the paper. It was an ancient volume, bound in cracked black leather and secured with two small iron locks. She'd found it as she was dusting.

Or rather, the book had found her. As Flan had poked her feather duster in and around the shelves in this long-forgotten corner of the shop, the book had quivered under her hand, nudging her until she finally tugged it from the shelf and cast a small latchkey spell to crack the locks.

The book was filled with handwritten notes, the ink faded by time. Flan ran her finger over the old-fashioned, hand-scribed text at the top of the page—The Transitory Enticement of Slumber. She drew in a quick breath. Transitory slumber. Could it be, could she have actually found—

Obsidian let out a low, throaty mewl. Flan rested a hand on his back, absently scratching him behind the ear to calm him. But Obsidian would not be calmed. His feline body arched. His silky fur bristled beneath Flan's hand. A shadow fell across the book, the pages fluttered, and a chill seemed to swallow the shop. Obsidian mewled again.

Flan held her place with her finger and dragged her gaze from the page, hoping to find a bookshop patron—someone needing an amulet, Uncle Anatole's advice, anything—standing in the open doorway.

But the doorway was empty, the front door still shut tight. She sighed and turned back to the book. The cat hissed at the bookshop door.

"Hush, Obsidian." Flan stroked his head and focused her attention on the spell in front of her: The Transitory Enticement of Slumber. She read through it once quickly, then again more slowly, savoring each word. Yes, it was as she first suspected, as she had hardly allowed herself to believe— she had discovered a most powerful sleep spell.

Slumber. To force sleep upon a powerful foe, let alone a group of foes, was a magic only the most skilled wizards ever attempted, a magic Uncle Anatole had warned her was too dangerous to try.

Flan sighed. Uncle thought everything was too dangerous. Left to him, she would never cast even the most harmless of household spells. Nay, left to him, she would concoct nothing stronger than plain black tea.

"It's not as if I go *looking* for magic," she muttered.

Obsidian let out a low growl.

"Fine. Perhaps I do go looking for it. But Uncle Anatole simply does not understand. Magic is beating in my heart, coursing through my veins. It is simply part of me." She shook her head. "The part Uncle would have me ignore."

The part Flan was finding it ever more difficult to ignore.

Flan had always known she was different. Different from her friends—what few she had left. Different even from Gwen, who had for so many years been so close as to almost be a sister. Different from anyone who lived on Wicker Street.

It wasn't simply that she'd been found in a basket. She rather liked that bit of her history. It lent a measure of adventure to her otherwise tame life, made her feel a little like one of the heroines in the adventure books she was always pulling from Uncle's bookshop shelves, gave her a certain glamour.

And it wasn't that she'd been named for a scrap of packing paper. She could have done worse. The innkeeper had named his daughter after his most beloved aunt—Ermintrude.

And it most assuredly wasn't that she'd grown up unloved. If anything, she'd grown up *too* loved. Uncle had cared for her, protected her, seen to her every need—including needs Flan was not convinced she truly needed at all. Twice-weekly boiled brussels sprouts sprang to mind.

No, it was none of those things . . . and all of them.

Anyone on Wicker Street could say who their parents were. They could identify their grandparents and great-grandparents and great-great-grandparents and uncles and cousins and cousins thrice removed. They could tell you which aunt they were named after, what side of the family their green eyes came from, who they got their great skill at horsemanship from. When they passed down their family stories, the stories became part of them, for their family's history was their history too.

But Flan's history only started the moment she'd been found at the bookshop door.

And fifteen years later, she found herself with a wild tangle of copper hair and a fiercely mulish streak. With magic tingling through every fiber of her being, more powerful than any on Wicker Street, perhaps even more powerful than Uncle's, if she were ever given free rein to hone her skills.

And with this longing to know why, how, where it had come from and no way to answer because Uncle refused to hear of it.

For most of her life Flan had tried to fit in, tried to be as normal as Gwen and the other girls on Wicker Street, tried to please her uncle and quash the magic that, despite her best efforts, refused to be quashed.

But she *didn't* fit in. She *wasn't* normal. She *did* possess magic—powerful magic—and pretending she didn't only made her feel even more of an outsider. As if she were an outsider even to herself.

Flan turned back to the crumbling page before her.

She read through the spell again, studying each line, each instruction, each word. "This makes much sense," she whispered to Obsidian, who had once again settled into a wary catnap. "I think it just might work."

For despite Uncle Anatole's warnings, Flan had secretly been trying out sleep spells for months. She would never hurt Uncle. Not purposely. But if she could send him into a slumber at will, she could do the things she needed to do, find things she needed to find, things that could, perhaps, lead her to the truth about her parents, her magic, herself, things Uncle never need know about.

"I would be doing him a favor," she told Obsidian. "Truly. With a sleep spell at my fingertips, I need never worry that someone may do me harm. I could simply send my foes into a restful slumber. It would harm no one, and would save Uncle the trouble of fretting over me."

The cat raised an eyelid and gave her a doubtful gaze.

Flan ignored him. "And save me the trouble of relying on another living soul. I could rely on myself alone, which is the smarter route to begin with."

Despite her best efforts, she had thus far met with little success. Oh, yes, there was the time she had managed to turn the feather duster a bit limp for the better part of an afternoon. And another when her spell had backfired and she'd dragged her own spell-numbed foot around the shop for a day. She wriggled her toes. On rainy days her foot still tingled from that small mishap. But most of her attempts were utter failures, resulting in nothing at all.

And suddenly, in front of her, was a long-forgotten sleep spell, a spell that had most likely not been attempted in decades, perhaps centuries, a spell that seemed, to Flan, to be both practical and logical.

"And safe," she told Obsidian. "Employing none of the volatile components that can turn a spell dangerous. No foxglove. No dragon's breath. No . . . black powder." She no more than whispered that last part. Uncle had so vehemently banished black powder from his shop and his magic that she scarcely dared think the words. "If anything, Uncle should approve."

Obsidian lifted an eyelid.

"Very well," said Flan. "Have it your way. Uncle would *not* approve. But you must allow, it is the sort of spell Uncle himself would craft. If, that is, he were still crafting spells."

She read the steps aloud, committing them to memory: "Mingle the essences of lavender for tranquility, caraway for mental vigor, and holly for safekeeping, preparing a tincture to fortify the spellcaster. Select four small mirrors. (The oval shape is the most reliable, as the circular shape may create excessive energy that can become burdensome to the spellcaster, while a shape with corners or angles can send the energy streaking off into unpredictable directions.) Place one mirror in the palm of each hand and in the bottom of each shoe, reflective side out . . ."

Flan was so lost in her magical world that she didn't notice the shadow, faint and fluttery, fall across the shop.

"Hallo?" A voice floated toward her.

Flan blinked, startled to find herself transported suddenly back to the world of bookshelves and feather dusters. She looked down to see the Wicker Street butcher standing in the open bookshop door, nervously kneading the cap in his hands.

"Master MacDougal. I didn't hear you come in." She scrambled from the ladder, eager to assist the butcher before he changed his mind and decided another wizard's shop might be more to his liking. "May I help you?"

A crisp breeze rippled in from the street beyond, swirling the butcher's feathery hair around his balding head as he nervously glanced around the shop. "These are Monsieur Anatole's, aren't they?" He pulled out a pair of spectacles. "I found them outside the door, on the window ledge. He must have misplaced them again."

Flan took the spectacles. One earpiece was bent from when he'd left them behind on the counter at the fishmonger's and an edge of the glass was singed and darkened from when he'd forgotten them on the cook stove.

Flan sighed. "Yes. They're his. I'll be sure he gets them. Thank you." Flan slipped the spectacles into the pocket of her frock and turned back to her spellbook.

The butcher cleared his throat.

Flan looked up. "Was there something else?"

Master MacDougal nervously glanced toward the door. "I didn't want to come here, but me wife, she insisted." He lowered his voice. "You see, something—or someone—has been sneaking into my shop at night."

Into his shop? Then he *had* come for magic, after all. Only the slightest bit of magic, most likely. Still, magic was magic. Flan's mind raced. Uncle was busy upstairs in his workshop, deep in his calculations. Perhaps she could help him herself. Uncle need never know.

She stole a glance at the jangle of amulets hanging from a peg by the counter. An amulet, yes. And a small warding spell. It would be good practice. She slid the spellbook under the counter.

"I wouldn't mind so much," the butcher was saying, "since this . . . this person, this creature, whatever it may be, this—this—"

"This intruder?" said Flan.

"Yes. This intruder." The butcher gave a grateful nod. "This intruder, he doesn't seem to be dangerous. Truth be known, he's more a help than a hindrance, swabbing up me butcher table, cleaning me knives, setting things to rights, cleaning up in general."

Flan frowned. Perhaps he wasn't in need of magic after all. She'd been to the butcher's shop. She'd wager that the butcher's burglar was most likely a housewife tired of brushing away flies when she stopped to buy a sausage, or a neighboring shopkeeper weary of the stench. But she wasn't about to turn away the first customer they'd had in well over three months. She could ward off a nettled housewife as well as any other creature.

"The only thing that's missing is me wife's old fiddle," the butcher was saying, "and with the way she plays it, I'm glad it's gone. Still it does set me teeth on edge, knowing someone's lurking around the shop. For well on a week now, me wife has tried all the small warding spells and herbal protections she knows. Failure, every one. Pure waste of the coin she spent buying the dragon's breath and salt. We're at our wits' end." He twisted the brim of his hat as he worked out the next bit in his head before he spoke. "I just want to be sure, I mean, seeing how things haven't always worked out with Monsieur Anatole, well"—he looked up—"I don't want to waste more of me hard-earned coin, if you take my meaning."

Flan sighed. She did take his meaning. She could not risk the butcher's hard-earned coin, nor his trust—nor the gossip that would race up and down Wicker Street if she made a mistake—on an untested spell of her own.

She gathered Obsidian into her arms. "I assure you your coin is safe," she told the butcher. "You were right to come to Uncle Anatole. You and your wife have suffered enough."

She subtly pointed a finger toward a velvet cord beside the shop's counter. The cord swished, ringing a bell upstairs in Anatole's workshop.

"Uncle will have your shop back to normal with so little fuss," she said, "you'll slap yourself for not coming sooner."

She gave the butcher a smile and led him to the narrow staircase to the rooms above.

Two

Flan burst into the parlor and found Uncle Anatole waiting before the hearth. A fire crackled behind him, casting a glow over his deep purple robes and adding an extra spark to his always fiery eyes.

She plucked the fine oaken wand from the umbrella stand beside the door.

"You may need this," she whispered as she handed the wand to her uncle. Then she stepped aside to allow the butcher to shuffle forth. "You remember Master MacDougal."

"Yes, of course." Anatole tipped his head, at once both gracious and regal. "Let us enjoy a bit of warmth and comfort as you explain what I may do for you." Anatole spread his arms toward the two chairs on either side of the fire.

"Thank you. I could do with a bit of comfort after the week I've had," the butcher said. "Makes you realize how defenseless we all really are these days. A thing like this never would've happened when Lord Blakely was still alive."

Lord Blakely! Simply hearing the name made Flan want to spit. Uncle would tell her it wasn't fair to blame a dead man—particularly a dead man who had only ever tried to help his townspeople while he still lived—for their own predicament. But Flan couldn't help herself. If Wicker Street would ever once stop worshiping the memory of Lord Blakely, perhaps they would notice the great source of protection living in their very midst, and perhaps Monsieur Anatole's Books, Wonders, and Charms would not sit moldering in its own dust. It vexed her that Uncle had to depend on their fickle Wicker Street neighbors for his livelihood. It vexed her that she and Uncle had to depend on anyone for anything.

The butcher settled into the near chair. He began describing his trouble, working his cap with such earnest that Flan thought the poor scrap of wool would scarcely survive the visit.

A slight snuffling noise on the mantelshelf above the butcher's head caught Flan's attention, and she drew in a sharp breath at the sight of Merlin, the hedgehog, curled in a spiny ball on the mantelshelf, fast asleep.

Her uncle did not seem to notice.

"So you say this intruder . . . cleans up?" Anatole asked the butcher.

Master MacDougal nodded. "Never seen me knives so shiny, not since I bought 'em brand new. And me work table, and the floor."

Flan edged behind the butcher's chair. She loved Merlin nearly as much as Anatole did, but the townspeople assumed that Obsidian, Flan's own cat, was the wizard's familiar. The nearsighted, nervous bundle of bristles above the hearth would hardly inspire confidence in the butcher—or anyone else who might think to seek her uncle's help—if they knew his true role.

Flan let Obsidian drop to the floor, free to curl himself around Anatole's legs—as the butcher no doubt supposed a good familiar would. She reached above the butcher, stretching to touch the mantelshelf. She ran her fingers along the timeworn wood—

—and nearly tipped a candlestick onto the butcher's head.

Bother. That would not do. Flan stole a glance at her uncle. He raised a sharp eyebrow at her and shook his head.

Flan sighed. The butcher was Uncle's first magic client in months. They'd only had a few customers in the shop—Wicker Street folk wandering in for a charm, the odd bit of bitterwort or dried fleabane, and, on rare occasions, a book. But clients seeking Monsieur Anatole's protection magic had dwindled to a trickle these past few years, until the trickle had dried to dust.

It was not Uncle's fault. Not in the beginning, at least. Flan remembered when Monsieur Anatole's Books, Wonders, and Charms was the centerpiece of Wicker Street, abuzz with customers night and day, when folk from Wicker Street and beyond clamored for Monsieur Anatole's spells, begged for his wise counsel.

That was before the blaze at the smithy's, of course. Before Uncle became so cautious.

Before he began spending all his time above stairs, conducting his experiments, inventing his contraptions, and otherwise pottering around his workshop.

"Wizardry is powerful, but so is science," he would tell her. "Think if I combined the two, Flan. There would be no limit to the good I could do in this world."

Uncle did not hear the whispers on the street, of course, nor see the looks that passed behind his back. "Monsieur Anatole has lost his way," people said. "Monsieur Anatole has lost his gift—if he ever had one. Perhaps we were wrong about him all along. Was he ever that great a wizard to begin with?" The townspeople, even their neighbors here on Wicker Street, had become more apt to either cross the city to consult a wizard a good hour's walk from home, or rely on their own small amount of protection magic than to spend the effort—and the coin—to consult Monsieur Anatole.

But unexpectedly, the Wicker Street butcher was asking for Uncle's help.

And asking in earnest. "It frazzles me nerves, I tell you. The missus, she didn't mind so much at first. She said it was high time somebody cleaned up around there."

Flan could not let one small hedgehog chase him off before Uncle had a chance to prove how much help he could be.

She ran a finger across her brow and, thinking to hide Merlin, surreptitiously pointed toward the pewter pitcher on the mantelshelf. The pitcher quivered. Flan crooked her finger, and the pitcher inched toward the hedgehog, making only a quiet scritch as it slid across the wood of the mantel.

The butcher, of course, did not notice anything out of the ordinary. "But it's my shop, and I tell you, it runs me blood cold knowing somebody's skulking around in there at night when I'm not around."

Uncle Anatole, of course, did notice. His face grew dark. He caught Flan's eye and gave a slight, nearly imperceptible shake of his head.

Merlin snuffled, louder this time. The butcher frowned and glanced around.

"Ah-ah-ah-choo." Flan let out her best false sneeze. "Oh, do excuse me. Something's been tickling my nose all day."

The butcher nodded and turned back to Monsieur Anatole. He had relaxed some small bit in the wizard's presence. He still gripped his cap tightly with both hands, but he had stopped twisting the bill.

"I lock the shop up tight every night," he said.

"Yes, of course," Anatole nodded. "Very wise."

Ever so slowly, ever so deliberately, Flan moved her finger to her face and scratched her nose. The pewter pitcher began, once again, to scrape along the mantelshelf.

"And I nailed the windows shut so's nothing could get in nor out," the butcher said.

Flan scratched. The pitcher scritched . . . to a halt. Flan frowned. She scratched again. The pitcher did not budge. She cast a glance at the mantel.

And caught a glimpse of her uncle. He sat in his snug chair before the hearth, listening to the butcher, leaning forward, eyes focused on the butcher's face, nodding at proper moments, to all appearances paying heed to nothing save the butcher's tale.

But Flan saw. She saw his hand, resting on the arm of his chair, forefinger raised toward the pitcher, unmoving, holding the pitcher in place. One muscle twitched above his eyebrow, the muscle that twitched at only one time—whenever he admonished her, once again, how dangerous it was for her to practice magic.

Vexation! It was but a small bit of summoning loco-motion. It hardly qualified as magic at all. Did Uncle not see the importance of it? Did he not understand that she was trying to keep Merlin from the butcher's view? That she was trying to help?

Flan raised her chin. She *would* help this time, whether Uncle wished it or not.

She took a deep breath, drew herself up to her full height, and, squeezing every amount of her attention on the pewter pitcher, crooked her finger. The pitcher began, at first, to slide toward her. But only for an instant, and then, as if caught on a nail or a rough patch on the wood, it lurched to a stop.

"Silly as it sounds, I even tried sleeping on the counter in the middle of me shop," the butcher was saying.

"Not silly at all, my good man. I'm certain I would have done the same." Anatole's voice cocooned the room like a soft, warm blanket, but his forefinger remained rigid, the muscle strained above his brow.

How stubborn he was! Flan narrowed her eyes and willed every bit of her magic into her finger. She pulled her finger toward her. The pitcher reeled.

"It helped not a whit," said the butcher. "The rascal managed to slip in, and me lying there in the middle of it, slumbering away like a newborn babe. Me wife gave me no small amount of grief over that one, I can tell you."

"I can only imagine." Anatole gave a warm chuckle but held his finger steady.

Flan pulled. Anatole pushed. The pitcher tipped precariously on the edge of the mantelshelf, directly above the butcher's head. Uncle Anatole's eyes grew stormy.

"Flannery." His great wizard voice boomed through the workshop, as well as the rooms beyond and possibly all of Wicker Street. His face was furrowed into a frown. "We've been most ill-mannered. We have not offered our guest refreshment."

Refreshment? Crone's nightgown. The first magic client to show up in months, and Uncle expected her to brew tea. Tea!

The butcher gave her a grateful smile. "Yes, thank you," he said. "Refreshment would be most welcome."

Of course it would be—for *him*. Flan sighed and dropped her hand. With a soft clink, the pitcher spun to a rest directly in front of Merlin, shielding the slumbering hedgehog from the butcher's view.

Uncle nodded and gave her a smile. Flan turned and stalked into the kitchen.

She quickly set to making a pot of chamomile tea. There was *some* sense in it, she allowed. The chamomile would settle the butcher's nerves, and the tea would give her uncle—and Flan, too, if she were being honest—a chance to puzzle out what, exactly, was going on each night in the butcher shop.

Uncle Anatole had designed an iron cooking stove long before Flan had come to live with him. A kettle of water had been steaming on its cooktop since breakfast. Flan rattled teapot, cups, and a tin of tea from the cupboard. She tapped her foot against the wood plank floor as she waited for the tea to steep, clanked the pot, teacups, and spoons onto a tray with a bowl of sugar and a small pitcher of milk, and carried the entire assembly into the workshop. She quickly served Master MacDougal and her uncle.

"Thank you, Flan." Uncle Anatole gave an approving nod. "Excellent choice. Most excellent. This will do nicely."

He rummaged in the pocket of his robes, frowned, then rummaged a bit more. Flan slid a hand into her own pocket and pulled out his spectacles—spectacles, Flan knew, that he had fashioned himself, making some good deal of improvement on the spectacles sold at the optician's.

"Is this what you're searching for?" She held out the eyeglasses.

"Ah, yes. Quite." Anatole took them and gave her a grateful smile.

"Master MacDougal brought them in," she said. "How you managed to mislay them on our front window ledge I can only guess."

Anatole slipped the spectacles onto his nose, where, as usual, they listed slightly to one side. Then he turned to the butcher. "I must thank you, my good sir. I would be lost without them."

The butcher nodded and began sipping his chamomile. Uncle Anatole took a bit more time, stirring his tea, seemingly lost in thought, to all appearances paying little attention to the cup in his hand.

But appearances were deceiving. Flan knew exactly what her uncle was doing, for she intended to do the same. She settled onto a three-legged stool and balanced the warm teacup on her knees. She stirred her tea. The steamy froth whirled, forming patterns—patterns that would give Flan a glimpse at the true nature of the butcher's intruder. The froth curled around itself, into the shape of a droplet.

Flan frowned. A droplet? Of what? Water, perhaps? A raindrop? She shook her head. What could a raindrop mean?

Uncle Anatole groaned and Flan glanced up. Uncle sat with his eyes closed, one hand pressed to his ear, the other clutching his spoon in such a desperate grip, Flan feared the silver would bend in half. As she watched, he opened his eyes, pulled the cup to him, and gave his tea a small, tentative stir. Immediately he sank back into his chair, eyes shut, head pressed against the cushion, face squeezed in anguish.

"Uncle?"

Anatole swallowed. His eyes fluttered open. "Yes, yes. I was simply—" He drew in a breath. "I was focusing my attention on Master MacDougal's problem. Trying to get a better picture. Master MacDougal." He peered at the butcher through his crooked spectacles. His pinched face began to relax. "You have no reason to fear. These creatures—"

"Creatures?" The butcher sat up straight in his chair. "There's more than one?"

"Yes. Yes." Anatole waved an impatient hand. "They tend to run in clusters, these little fellows. You'd be hard pressed to find one by himself. But they pose no danger to you or your wife. They are brownies. Common household brownies."

Flan's frown deepened. Brownies? She stirred her tea, but the froth simply swirled and melted away, telling her nothing. Brownies. If the tea had foreseen brownies, the froth would have formed the shape of a star, not a droplet. How had she missed it? It made little sense. Brownies were vegetarian. The carnage of the butcher shop would repulse them. They would want the mess cleaned up, certainly. But they would not be the ones to do it.

"Yes, well. It's good we have that problem solved then." Anatole rose from his chair, as if to show Master MacDougal the door.

But the butcher remained firmly planted in his chair. He frowned. "So how do I get rid of them, then?"

Anatole shrugged. "There's really no need. They're useful, these brownies, as you've discovered for yourself. They finish up any housework left undone at the end of the day, and they make a tidy job of it. Not a bad trade for a small nighttime snack. I've known folk who leave sweets out at night, trying to lure them in." He patted Master MacDougal's shoulder, as if to coax him from the chair. "I'm glad we could settle your trouble with so little fuss."

"No, sir." The butcher gave a firm shake of his head. "It's my shop, and these brownies weren't invited. I want them gone."

Anatole frowned. "Are you certain?"

Master MacDougal gave a firm nod. "I am, sir."

Anatole dropped his arm. "Very well." Reluctantly, Anatole reached deep within the pocket of his robes. He pulled out a small object. "This amulet should resolve your brownie troubles nicely."

He set the amulet onto the hearth.

"That's what you call an amulet?" The butcher said.

Flan's heart sank. The amulet was nothing more than a bar of plain metal, dangling from a rough leather cord, its only embellishment a single strand of copper, twisted round the bar from top to bottom.

Little wonder the butcher looked disappointed. It was nothing like the lavishly adorned charms and talismans displayed in the shop below.

Flan knew Uncle had been trying to fuse his magic with his science. She assumed the copper wire was the scientific aspect in this case. It would undoubtedly give the amulet more power.

But couldn't Uncle have tried to make it *look* more powerful? The butcher already seemed more than a little unsure about coming here. Uncle could have gone a long way toward reassuring Master MacDougal simply by using a more elaborate amulet.

Flan sighed. If *she* were allowed to run the shop, she would make sure her clients received the full effect of her magic. She would create wondrous and breathtaking amulets and infuse them with wondrous and breathtaking wizardry in a wondrous, breathtaking, and theatrical manner. Her clients would leave the shop knowing, beyond any doubt, that they were protected by a most powerful magic indeed. She would not have to rely on their fickle nature, wheedle herself into their good graces. She would never need trust in another soul for her livelihood. She would never need trust another soul for anything. Her reputation would be so great, clients would simply clamor for her magic.

Except that, of course, she would never *have* clients. Uncle had so stubbornly insisted that she never practice her magic, never mention her magic, not even to her closest friends, not even to Gwen, that no one had an inkling she possessed even the slightest magical power. As far as Wicker Street knew, Flan was no more magical than a simple serving girl.

Anatole lifted his wand. Its finely carved oaken shaft gleamed in the firelight. Its deep green jade orb seemed to glow from within. Holding it, Monsieur Anatole seemed taller somehow, bigger than the steadfast uncle and sympathetic neighbor who'd sat stirring his tea only moments before. His robes billowed. His hair flowed. His fingertips fairly crackled with electricity. The very air around him seemed different, charged with energy and expectation. Even the fire in the hearth seemed ready to obey him, the flames leaping higher now, licking the stones at the base of the chimney.

Anatole trained the wand at the amulet. He drew in a breath and began to recite the ancient runes that would cast the spell. "*YOU-et.*" The plain metal bar began to glow a warm orange. "*VEE—VEE . . .*"

Anatole's voice sputtered to a halt. He closed his eyes and held his hand to his temple. The oaken wand faltered. The amulet's metal bar dimmed to its customary dull gray.

"Uncle?" Flan sat forward.

"Is something wrong?" The butcher frowned.

"No—I—" Anatole opened his eyes. "I was taken away momentarily by the strength of the spell. Let us begin again."

The great wizard raised his arms once more. He drew himself up and focused his wand on the amulet.

"YOU-et, VEE—ah!" Anatole doubled over, both hands clutching his head, his spectacles askew. His great oaken wand clattered to the wide stone hearth.

"Uncle!" Flan rushed to his side. "Are you—?"

"Fine, Flan, dear." Anatole reached for his errant wand. "I am entirely fine."

Flan studied her uncle's face. He most certainly was *not* fine. His usually fiery eyes were now as dull as the ashes in the fireplace grate. His forehead was creased in pain. His great wizardly voice had thinned to a rasp, and his robes drooped over shoulders that suddenly felt thin.

Flan heard a scuttling on the mantel and looked up to find that Merlin had uncurled himself from his slumber and had poked a fretful nose out from his hiding place behind the pewter pitcher. Even Anatole's familiar had become anxious.

The butcher rose to his feet. "This was a mistake. Me wife insisted, but I should have known." He stalked to the door. "It's only more of what Wicker Street has been saying for years. This just adds to the list."

Adds to the list? Flan stared at him. The butcher would tell everyone. He *would* add to the list, to the growing list of rumors and gossip that swirled around Wicker Street whenever Antole's name was mentioned, and Uncle—and his shop—would be even worse off than they already were.

"No." Flan ran after him. "You can't go."

"Flan." Her uncle's voice was little more than a croak. "If Master MacDougal wishes to leave, we cannot stop him."

But Flan *could* stop him. She had to.

"Please, Master MacDougal," she said. "Uncle is only—"

"Only a doddering old fool, is what he is." The butcher thrust his cap on his head. "And I was a fool to think any different."

"You're wrong." Flan grasped at the butcher's sleeve. "He's done nothing—"

"Nothing! You're right about that, lassie." He shook her hand loose. "Nothing that ever came to any good, anyway. And you." He shook a fat sausage finger in her face. "You're no better, luring folk in with false claims."

"False claims?" Flan jerked back, as if she'd been slapped. "I never—"

"'Your coin is safe,' you say. 'You and your wife have suffered enough,' you say. 'Uncle will fix you up so quick, you'll slap yourself for not coming sooner.'" The butcher reached for the door handle. "Well, we can see how that turned out, can't we?"

"But you never gave him a chance—"

"Next you'll be telling me you have the magic too."

"I do! I'm more powerful than you know. I could take care of your brownies in a snap." Flan heard her voice ring out before she even realized she'd spoken.

Three

The butcher stared at her in surprise.

"Flan." Uncle had slipped in behind her, and his voice sounded as horrified as Flan felt.

The butcher raised an eyebrow. "You've lived here all your life, Flannery Lane, grew up under me very nose, never showed one glimmer of magic, and now you'll have me believe you have great magical powers?" He shook his head, gave Anatole a scathing look, and reached for the door. "A less magical girl would be hard to imagine."

Less magical? Flan set her jaw. Her wand finger twitched. She would show the Wicker Street butcher precisely how non-magical this girl happened to be.

"Flan." Anatole clamped a hand on her shoulder, his voice low and filled with stern warning.

But setting the butcher's cap ablaze would do Uncle little good. She sighed and tucked her hands into the pocket of her frock, where her wand finger could do no mischief.

"Master MacDougal, wait." She took a breath, gathered her wits about her, and managed to smile her most gracious smile. "You misunderstand me. My—my magic is in the way I—I tend the shop, tend our rooms here above, tend to my uncle, keeping him unencumbered by mundane daily tasks so that he is free to concentrate on his magic. *I* am the one who made the mistake, not my uncle."

Once Flan began her explanation, it rather rolled off her tongue. The butcher had dropped the door handle and turned to listen to her, she noticed, and she thought that her greatest magic might be concocting tales to explain it.

"I should have mentioned it when you first arrived," she said. "Uncle is bone weary. He has not slept in days. Each night, as he drifts into slumber, a great racket awakens him. Scritching and scratching and all manner of . . . how did you describe it, Uncle? Didn't you say it sounded like scrubbing?"

The butcher narrowed his eyes. "Scrubbing?"

Flan nodded. "I don't hear this scrubbing, of course, nor any of the racket, but then, I wouldn't, would I?" She swallowed, for she did not believe she was about to utter these words. "I do not possess Uncle's great powers. For it is plain that he has been sensing your dilemma, Master MacDougal. He's been worried about you."

"Me, you say?" The butcher cocked a look at Anatole.

"Yes." Flan continued before her uncle could speak. "He has divined your trouble. His powers are so great that he was able to hear their mischief-making, even in his dreams. It's been going on for nigh on a week now."

The butcher's eyes widened. "Nigh on a week? That's when it started exactly." He turned an admiring gaze on

Uncle Anatole. "Me wife, she said you would help. Forgive me, I had me doubts. But—"

Flan waved a hand. "Of course you did. Perhaps now we should allow Uncle to continue."

She led the butcher back into the parlor. Anatole settled in once again to charm the butcher's amulet. His great robes billowed. His white hair flowed. The color had returned to his cheeks, the ashen gray from before only a memory.

Still—Flan narrowed her eyes—something was amiss. Uncle's lips were pressed into a thin line. He gripped his wand as he stroked the phoenix feathers at his belt.

Flan frowned. Uncle only rubbed the feathers when he was worried about something. Very worried. The plain metal bar still lay on the hearth, and Uncle gave it a suspicious look, as if he did not trust it.

Flan felt the worry bubble up in her own throat. He did not want to spell the amulet. She had never seen her uncle reluctant to do magic, but he hesitated. Whatever had happened the first time he'd tried must have been more distressing than she realized. Her gaze darted around the parlor, seeking something—anything—that would tell her what to do.

Her gaze landed on Merlin—and the pewter pitcher. She turned to Anatole.

"Uncle," she said, "is there anything you want? Anything *YOU-et* need?" She discreetly traced the rune for protection—*YOU-et*—in the air with her finger. "A pitcher"—she allowed her gaze to flick to the mantel—"of . . . water perhaps?"

Anatole followed her gaze. He studied the pitcher. "Yes," he said at last. "*YOU-et* may help with the pitcher. But only this once."

Flan skittered into the kitchen for a drinking glass and pitcher of water. As Uncle made a show of pouring water into his glass and taking a long refreshing swallow, Flan faded into the shadows behind the butcher's chair.

"You were right in coming, Master MacDougal." Anatole set the pitcher and drinking glass on the table and drew himself up to his full wizardly height. "Rest assured, I will be able to help you. Shall we begin again?"

The butcher perched on the edge of his chair and gave an eager nod. If he noticed that Monsieur Anatole held the magnificent oaken wand in the wrong hand, he gave no sign. Behind the butcher, unseen, Flan slid a hand into the pocket of her frock and pulled out a slender hazel twig, no bigger than a pencil, twisted round with a thin ribbon of silver satin—the only sort of wand her uncle would permit her to have.

The wizard raised his arms.

Behind the butcher, Flan raised hers. A soft, disapproving growl rumbled in Obsidian's throat. Merlin huffled and snorted.

"Hush. Both of you," Flan whispered.

As Anatole flourished his wand—at nothing in particular—Flan flourished her hazel twig directly toward the amulet. The plain metal bar quivered against the hearthstone.

"The tricks and the mischief and chaos must stop." Anatole's voice, clear and steady, filled the parlor.

Flan blinked. She had never heard Uncle utter *those* words before. She was fairly certain he was making them up on the spot. But they would do as well as any other, and in any case, the butcher seemed thoroughly convinced. His eyes gleamed in rapt admiration.

As her uncle spoke, Flan, unheard by the butcher, murmured the true words to the spell, the ancient runes: "*YOU-et. VEE-ex. TWO-zee.*" She held the hazel twig low and traced the wandwork. The gray metal bar began to glow a deep orange.

"Repel the young rascals—"

Anatole held his wand steady. Flan focused her hazel twig.

"—from MacDougal's fine shop."

The strand of copper wrapped round the amulet began to glimmer. A blue spark of energy sizzled up the length of the copper and set off a small pop at the end.

As the tiny pillow of smoke cleared, Anatole raised an eyebrow at Flan. She gave a slight nod. Anatole smiled. Flan slipped the hazel twig back into her pocket.

"Here you are, my friend." Anatole retrieved the amulet, slid it into a small velvet pouch, pulled the drawstrings taut, and handed it to the butcher. "Hang this inside your door at night after you have locked the shop up tight. You should have no further trouble. Take care to handle it only by the leather cord. The magical energy is conducted along the copper strand, and the amulet itself can become quite warm."

"Thank you, Monsieur." The butcher clutched the pouch to his chest. "I'll run straightaway to safeguard my shop." He pulled a handful of coins from his pocket and pressed them into Anatole's gloved hand. "Thank you."

The butcher scooted through the stairway door and clattered down the stairs, not waiting for Flan to see him out.

Flan closed the door behind him.

"Uncle." She turned to Anatole. "What was—"

She stopped. Her uncle stood before the hearth, one trembling hand directing his wand toward the fire, the other hand pressed to his ear, as he traced the wandwork of a simple scrying spell, murmuring the runes beneath his breath.

"*EN-mur.*" His voice was barely a rasp. "*FA-we*—ah!"

The great oaken wand clattered to the hearth.

Anatole collapsed onto the rug.

Four

Uncle!"

Flan scrambled to Anatole's side.

"I'm—I'm fine—Flan. I'm—fine." Anatole raised himself onto one elbow. The blue of his veins stood out in sharp contrast against the chalky white of his face.

Flan braced her hands under his arm and helped him sit up. "You're clearly *not* fine."

She gathered his still-full teacup from the table, cast a small heating spell to warm it, and held it to his lips.

"What happened?" She held the cup steady. "Are you ill?"

Anatole took a long sip of tea. "Ill." He harrumphed. "If only it were that simple."

He set down the teacup and struggled to his feet, leaning heavily on the arm of the chair. Merlin snuffled and skittered on the mantel above him, and Anatole gathered the nervous hedgehog into his arms before sinking into the chair. Merlin was but a small bristled ball in the wizard's immense gloved hands. Anatole held him close and stared into the fire as he stroked the hedgehog's spines—whether to calm Merlin or to calm himself, Flan could not say.

She pressed her palm against her uncle's forehead. She felt no fever. In truth, his skin was so unnaturally cold and damp, it was like laying her palm against a clay slab.

"Flan. Please." Anatole batted her hand away. "I am not an invalid."

"No. But something is clearly wrong. You can't pretend it isn't."

Anatole said nothing. He pulled his deerskin gloves from his hands and laid them on the table at his side.

Flan stood watching him. Frustration burned her throat. "You wouldn't have allowed me to complete the protection spell unless something was very wrong."

Anatole closed his eyes. "If you must know." He pushed his spectacles to his forehead and pinched the bridge of his nose. "I couldn't complete the spell because"—He raised a hand to his ear—"I was overwhelmed."

"Overwhelmed?" Flan frowned. "By what?" She began gathering up teacups and spoons, more to give her hands something to do than because of a sudden enthusiasm for tidiness.

"Bells."

"Bells?" Flan nearly dropped the cups in her hands.

Anatole shook his head. "It sounds peculiar, I grant you. How can the chime of a bell harm anyone, much less a full-grown wizard? But these were not chiming bells, Flan. It was if I were standing amongst the enormous carillon bells in the Grand Street clock tower." He rubbed a finger over his eye. "The more I tried to withstand them, the louder they tolled. The louder they tolled, the weaker I became, to the point where, shamefully, these—these *bells* brought me to my knees." Anatole's face creased in anguish.

"There's no shame in it, Uncle." Flan ached to throw her arms around his neck and give him a reassuring hug, but she knew he would only bat her away again. Instead, she collected the butcher's empty cup. "It's not something you could help."

"There *is* shame in it, Flan." Anatole thumped a weak fist against the arm of the chair. "For a wizard to be rendered powerless by the tolling of a bell? It's humiliating."

He sank back into the cushions, and at once Flan's strong, steadfast uncle, the grand wizard who had, less than an hour before, been bursting with fervor over a nearly perfected message chute, seemed . . . frail. Flan looked away. She could not bear to see him that way.

Flan deposited the tea things in the kitchen and took a moment to coax more warmth into the rooms. She kneeled before the squat iron heating stove, rattled the latch free, and gave a tug on the handle. The door protested, but at last swung open with a reluctant screech. Heat billowed out and nearly singed Flan's brows.

She stepped back and grabbed Uncle's iron poker. The embers inside had burned down to a few specks of dull orange within a pile of ash. As Flan jabbed them with the poker, a shower of sparks rained from the opening. She waved them away, slid two hedge logs into the stove, and latched the door shut again. She brushed her hands together and gave a satisfied nod. The logs would soon catch fire, heating the enormous vat of water above it and forcing the steam through the great pipes that snaked up the walls, crisscrossed the ceiling, and disappeared into the plaster and brick to carry hot steam to their living quarters and the shop below.

While most of the shops along Wicker Street remained dank and drafty throughout the long winter months, the bookshop remained snug all year. The townspeople believed Monsieur Anatole had charmed his establishment, casting a spell to keep it warm. It certainly guaranteed more customers during the long winter months, although they were hardly there to shop. They huddled in the bookshop on particularly frigid days, soaking up the warmth, completely unaware that the heat came from well-hidden steam pipes behind the walls and shelves, not from Anatole's magic.

Once Flan had suggested that perhaps it would be better to do away with the complicated snarl of pipes and heat the shop with magic. But Anatole dismissed the idea out of hand.

"Pah," he had said. "Magic is easy. It is engineering that is hard. Providing warmth and comfort for an entire house, using only a hedge wood fire, a water tank, and a few lengths of pipe—now *that* is a demonstration of greatness."

It was his fondest wish that his fellow shopkeepers—who tended to cling to the old ways, trusting magic more than anything new—would one day accept his steam-heat system so that all of Wicker Street could enjoy such comfort.

Flan sighed and returned to the parlor. She found her uncle slumped in his chair.

She kneeled beside him. "Your magic is still there, Uncle. It's just being . . . obstructed, somehow, by these bells. And in any case, they haven't blocked all your magic. You were able to scry the butcher's brownies in your teacup. The bells did not stop you there."

Anatole said nothing. He sat in the chair, staring at the fire. Merlin snuffled his small black nose into Anatole's palm, and Anatole stroked him absently.

Flan studied his face. "You did scry the butcher's brownies in your teacup. Did you not?"

Anatole waved an impatient hand. "I hardly needed to scry the swirling steam of my tea to identify the cause of the butcher's troubles. Any roustabout on the street could have told Master MacDougal he was infested with brownies. Unseen intruders, able to enter a locked shop without difficulty, leaving the place spit-spot clean in the morning— it hardly requires magic."

Flan frowned. "But you did *try* to scry in your teacup. I saw you."

Anatole closed his eyes. "Yes. I did try." His entire body seemed to deflate before Flan's eyes. "That's when it started."

He ran a hand through his wisp of white hair.

"No," he said, "that is not when it began. If we're being truthful, it began with the fire at the blacksmith's. It did something to me, Flan. I tried to believe it didn't, but I've only been deceiving myself. This is simply the final blow."

"What do you mean, the final blow? It has nothing to do with the blacksmith and nothing to do with our dwindling clients. You can't think—Uncle, this isn't your magic breaking down."

"I'm old, Flan."

"And wizards begin hearing bells when they age? I've never heard of that before."

"Ah. Well." He gave her a pointed look, and a bit of the spark seemed to shine through the dullness of his eyes. "Since you are suddenly so wise, what would you have me believe?"

Flan shook her head. "Perhaps you're ill, Uncle. Perhaps you were suffering a fever."

He raised an eyebrow. "So wizards begin hearing bells when they fall ill? I've never heard of *that* before."

Flan sighed. "Perhaps not, but there must be some explanation. Your magic can't simply have faded away. I cannot believe that."

"No." Anatole sat for a moment, stroking Merlin's quills. "I cannot believe it either. I can think of only one other explanation, an explanation I also do not want to believe."

Flan blinked. "You mean—"

Anatole nodded. "A curse."

"But how?" Flan frowned. "And why? Who would want to do you harm?"

Her uncle shrugged. "The blacksmith has no great love for me."

"But the blacksmith has no magic with which to curse you."

"True enough." Anatole stared into the fire. "But he could hire someone who does."

Hire someone? Flan began to pace the room. Gwen would never allow her father to do such a terrible thing. Would she? Then again, Gwen hadn't spoken to them in years. Flan barely knew her anymore.

"There is only one thing left to do." Anatole sat for a moment, lost in thought, then reached for his wand and, using it as a sort of cane, lifted his bone-weary body from the chair.

He tucked Merlin, now asleep, into the pocket of his robes and shuffled across the parlor. From one of the shelves, Anatole pulled a thick leather-bound book, its cover darkened by time and use. He blew dust from a corner of his work table and settled the book onto the cleared spot. The lamplight flickered over its richly engraved leather. A single ruby embedded in the cover cast a crimson glow across the work table.

The book was his grimoire, and it had been a long time since Flan had seen him use it.

He leafed through the pages until he found the one he sought, then sank back into his chair and closed his eyes. Flan read the page upside down: *Protectus Maximus*. She frowned. It seemed to be some sort of potion. A highly powerful potion of protection.

Anatole tapped the page and looked up at Flan. "This is it, Flan. It has to be. We have everything we need save two ingredients." With his phoenix feather pen, he scratched a note onto a scrap of parchment and handed it to Flan. "Fetch these and return quickly."

Flan scanned the short list. "But Uncle. This says"—she looked up—"black powder."

Anatole nodded.

Flan's heart fluttered. "But what about the fire at the smithy's? You said—"

"I know what I said, Flan, but we have no other choice. We'll just have to take our chances that, this time, nothing will go wrong."

Five

F lan hurried along the alleyway, her black laced boots clicking along the cobblestones, her cape whipping around her legs. She pulled the hood of her cape up over her head to ward off the cold—and the curiosity of any merchant or beggar who chanced to notice her.

She had escaped through the back of the bookshop, wriggling through a small window that opened onto the alley, a window that, under normal circumstances, Uncle Anatole did not like her to use.

Today, however, even Uncle agreed she should take the least conspicuous route from the shop. She needed to be quick, she needed to be discreet, and she did not need Wicker Street knowing where she was going or why. If anyone suspected what she was after, she and Uncle would be run out of Wicker Street before night fell. Anatole had given her moonstones to slip into each shoe to ensure a safe journey. Flan hoped it would be enough.

She clutched the parchment he had given her tightly in her mittened hand. Willow bark and black powder, scrawled in Uncle's nearly illegible handwriting. The willow bark was a simple ingredient, one she'd fetched for her uncle many times before. She knew exactly where to find it. But black powder? She looked at the list again and the address scratched beneath it. Should she really let him do this? She stuffed the paper in her cloak pocket.

Flan skittered down the narrow, murky alley. The upper floors of the shops jutted out into the alleyway above her on either side, blocking out all hope of the sun's morning rays breaking through. She blew warm breath into her fisted hands and hurried on, head bent, eyes fixed on the stone walk directly in front of her.

She had scarcely journeyed two blocks from the shop, had not even left the familiar confines of Wicker Street, when she heard a rasping sound.

She stopped, mittened hand against the rough brick, and heard it again—someone breathing heavily, as if trying to catch his breath. She peered through the gloom.

At the end of the alley, she spied a tall silhouette of black against the early morning light of the lane beyond.

He stood with his back pressed against the alley wall, his chest heaving, his quick breath floating out in white puffs against the light. He had pushed the collar of his dark top-coat back from his face, and Flan could see the outline of features, fine and sharply chiseled. His long curled eyelashes fluttered with each rasping breath.

She squeezed tight to the brick wall.

So intent was she on not being seen that she didn't realize she had reached the back doorway of the White Mane

Tavern—and the jumble of boxes and kegs that Mr. Jenks, the tavern keep, had heaped in the alleyway beside it.

As she sidled along, she banged her toe square against an empty ale keg. The keg tipped. Flan clapped a hand over her mouth to stifle the squeal of pain that bubbled up from her throat and threw out an arm to catch the pile of boxes sliding toward her.

But she had startled a fat orange cat from the depths of the heap. Flan recognized the cat in an instant. It was Miss Nibbles, the butcher's annoying orange tabby, who could not seem to stop herself from picking cat fights with Obsidian.

Miss Nibbles yowled, leaped from the dark insides of the keg, and darted away in a banging and clanging of buckets, barrels, and crates. An ale bottle rolled under Flan's feet. She skittered and flailed and finally landed with a hard thump on the pavement.

She lay on the cold cobblestones, eyes closed, not knowing whether she could even draw a breath, but certain that she did not want to try.

"Miss?"

Flan peeled her eyelids open. The mysterious silhouette from the end of the alleyway was watching her, except that he was no longer a silhouette, and he was no longer at the end of the alley. He was solid and three-dimensional, and he stood over her, directly above her head, so that when she opened her eyes, she found herself looking at his chin upside down.

"Are you injured?"

"Oh. No." Flan was relieved to find that she could, in fact, draw enough breath to speak. "I'm fine. A bit clumsy."

She pushed herself up onto her elbows. "But otherwise unharmed."

The stranger offered his elbow, but Flan pretended not to notice. She was not an invalid, or worse, a simpering, helpless girl. She was perfectly capable of dragging her own bruised and humiliated body from the rubble of the alleyway. She struggled to a sitting position, but when she tried to climb to her feet, her boot slipped on the pebbles, and she landed—hard—once more on her backside.

The stranger peered down at her. "You're certain you don't need a hand?"

Flan raised her chin. "I'm quite all right, I tell you."

The stranger tipped his head, as if considering this. "Accepting help means accepting a certain amount of vulnerability, I grant you. But you've nothing to fear from the sleeve of my coat." He placed his hand over his heart. "You have my word on it."

He gazed down at her with such a solemn expression on his upside-down face, his lovely lips curling ever so slightly at the corners, that Flan had to laugh. With a defeated sigh, she reached for his elbow. And as she grasped it and allowed him to help her to her feet, she couldn't help noticing that beneath the fine wool of his topcoat, his arm felt quite strong.

Which was utterly ridiculous—and exactly what a simpering, helpless girl would notice.

She dropped his arm and brushed the gravel from her skirt. She pushed her hair from her face, and arranged her face into a smile, prepared to give the stranger proper thanks— the price of accepting his help. But when she looked up, the words tumbled into a logjam in her throat. She opened her mouth, but nothing came out.

The stranger was tall, and strong, yes, but slender, his messy black hair falling into his eyes. He looked no older than Flan herself. His pale eyes met hers, and Flan felt all logical thought flee from her mind.

"I—" She swallowed. "I need—I mean—I *want* to—"

"Thank me?" He smiled, and the corners of his eyes crinkled in amusement. "There's no need. Your continued safety is the only thanks I require."

He lifted her hand in his. Her knitted mittens seemed an ungainly mound of nubbly wool against his sleek leather riding gloves, but he appeared not to notice. The scent of him swirled around her like a spicy clean cloud. He leaned over her hand and gave it a whisper of a kiss.

For a moment she forgot to breathe. She closed her eyes. When she opened them again, he was gone.

Six

Flan stood for a moment, hand raised absurdly in front of her, staring at the spot where, only a moment before, the stranger had stood.

At the end of the alleyway, she thought she caught a quick movement, perhaps a flicker of messy black hair, flutter around the corner.

Before she knew what she was doing, she found her boots clacking along the cobblestones after him. What harm would it be to follow him? She hadn't properly thanked him, after all. It was only polite.

When she reached the end of the alleyway, she slowed her steps and took in a deep breath. But when she turned the corner, the broad boulevard was empty of passersby.

She blinked. Where had he gone?

She'd bumped her head when she'd fallen, but surely not hard enough to begin inventing strangers in alleyways—strangers who kissed her hand, no less.

Still she could not help thinking about the stranger's lovely pale eyes.

Lovely pale eyes? Crone's nightgown! Flan gave herself a shake. She was becoming as empty-headed as the Wicker Street girls who swooned over any bachelor, no matter how ill-mannered or dim. If Gwen were here, she would tell her she'd been reading too many tales of adventure.

Flan straightened her skirts, righted her hood, and set off at a brisk pace down the boulevard. She had willow bark to collect, and not a great deal of time in which to collect it.

As she approached Blakely Manor, Flan pushed her hood back just enough to afford herself a better view.

The estate had been abandoned many years before, but the townspeople never tired of repeating the legend. It had been embellished along the way with so many exaggerated details—each more riveting than the last—that Flan could never be certain that she had sifted fact from fiction. She only knew that the tale was more adventurous than any she'd read in Uncle's shop.

Xander Blakely, the last Viscount Blakely, was a champion of the city, fiercely protective of his townspeople, highly skilled in the defensive arts, with particular expertise in hunting down all manner of foul being—monster, werewolf, vampire, fiend. While he lived, the townspeople felt safe. They knew no evil would come near their city, not while the great Lord Blakely resided in the great manor house.

But that was before the duel, a duel fought, according to Wicker Street, over a woman.

"A seamstress, of all people!" Flan had heard the butcher's wife say more than once. She told the story every year on the anniversary of Lord Blakely's death. "Or an embroiderer.

Perhaps a quilt maker. From over in the old textiles market below Blakely Manor. A commoner," she sniffed.

Which amused Flan to no end, since Mrs. MacDougal and everyone else on Wicker Street—in truth, nearly everyone in the city—were commoners as well.

As was the snake who had betrayed Lord Blakely: Lucien Kidd, the viscount's closest boyhood friend.

"Never knew his place, that one," Mrs. MacDougal said. "Nothing more than the Blakely stablemaster's son, playmate of young Blakely as a boy and puffed-up enough to think he was Xander's equal when they were grown. Never happy with his station in life. I heard him say more than once he'd sooner burn the Blakely stable to the ground than tend the horses there."

On the eve of Xander Blakely's wedding, Lucien Kidd had challenged the viscount to a duel.

"Wanted his lordship's commoner bride for himself, he did," Mrs. MacDougal would say.

But Lucien Kidd was no match for Xander Blakely, and the viscount soon had the better of him. Lucien, angry and humiliated, fled the city. No one heard of him for nearly a year. The townsfolk all but forgot him.

But Lucien Kidd did not forget the city, nor his feud with Xander Blakely. When he returned years later, he was, in many ways, completely unchanged. He was still angry. He was still hotheaded. He was still unwilling to forget old wounds.

But in one way, the most important way, he could not have changed more. For Lucien Kidd was now one of the undead. He was a vampire. A vengeful vampire. His anger had boiled into rage, and he returned bent on destroying the man he believed had destroyed him. The two fought once more in a vicious battle that raged from the grounds of the manor all the way to the top of the manor house. And this time, Lucien got the upper hand. Xander was killed. Lucien was never seen again. Nor was Xander Blakely's bride.

The manor fell into disrepair, and along with it, the safety the townspeople felt. With Lord Blakely gone, they suddenly—and for the first time anyone could remember—felt vulnerable to evil.

Flan kicked at a pebble on the boulevard. The townspeople would have done better to worry less about the evil that might be done to them and more about the evil they had done.

While their great protector still lived, Monsieur Anatole had been a respected wizard running a respectable shop. He was well known for his gifts in all manner of protection magic, and while the people of Wicker Street trusted in Lord Blakely to keep true evil at bay, they relied upon Anatole for small daily safeguards. But when Lord Blakely died, fear and desperation drove the town—in throngs—to Monsieur Anatole. Monsieur Anatole's Books, Wonders, and Charms became the beating heart of Wicker Street.

Flan did not remember Uncle's overnight success, of course, for she was but a baby then. But she certainly remembered what a lively place the bookshop had been as she was growing up. As Flan clattered past Blakely Manor, she allowed the warm memories to flood over her. Uncle had truly been in his element then, the grand master of Wicker Street. People crowded through the bookshop doors from morning till night seeking his amulets, his spells, his advice.

And Gwen came to the shop nearly every day. Flan and Gwen found no end of hiding places in the bookshop: beneath the work counter, between the shelves, behind the staircase, even perched atop Uncle's rolling bookshelf ladder. Monsieur Anatole's customers took little notice of two young girls prowling underfoot.

And then the night of the fire, everything had changed.

Flan pulled the hood of her cloak closer. She hurried alongside the Blakely estate, her breath coming out in small white puffs that hung in the cold, gray afternoon air.

She had felt cold since she left the bookshop, a nagging, tolerable sort of cold. But as Flan passed the great house, a sharp chill shot through her. She looked up and, just as she did every time she passed by, drew in a sharp breath at the sight of it—at the great stone fortress standing tall and unmoving on a rise overlooking the city.

But then she drew in a second breath, even sharper than the first. For something was different about the crumbling manor —she could see it, actually *see* it, the whole thing, not just the roofs and parapets peeking out above the tangle of weeds and brush that had grown up around it. She could see the great front door, the ornate iron fence around the court-yard. Someone had cleared the lawns and dammed the small stream that ran through the estate.

Odd, she thought, for as far as she knew, Lord Blakely had died without heirs. There had been rumors that distant

Blakely kinsmen still lived in far-off lands, but in all these years, none had come forward to claim the estate. Certainly none had ever taken notice of the rotting old manor house.

Flan stared up at the manor's stone walls—magnificent even as their edges crumbled to dust. She wondered, yet again, what life must have been like behind them. Had Lord Blakely's bride—the seamstress!—felt as small and insignificant standing before these great iron gates as Flan did now? Had she reveled in the lavishness of her new life as a viscountess, or had she felt isolated, cut off from her old life in the city?

She shook her head. She had no time for fantasies about life as a great lady. She had much to do and little time to do it.

Flan came to a narrow bridge where the iron fence dipped away from the boulevard. There the small stream that wound through the back of the estate had always burbled out from beneath the fence and under the bridge, winding its way through the city before spilling into the great river that roared past the clock tower. But since it had been dammed higher up the hill, the stream was scarcely more than a trickle.

She glanced around, to make sure no fellow traveler on the boulevard was near enough to see, then scrambled down the bank and along the stream, her boots squelching through the spongy ground. She squeezed through the fence where the rusting iron bars rose to let the stream flow through and slipped into the stand of willow trees beyond. She glanced around again, to be sure no one had seen—or followed—then slid a small knife from her boot.

She chose a large tree near the water and shaved off several chunks of its curling bark. As she slid the bark into her string bag, a sharp breeze whistled through the willow grove. Through the bare winter branches she could see the manor house, the somberness of the stone nearly disappearing into the misty gloom of the sky, the entire scene a still, unrelenting gray.

Except—

Flan looked closer.

—except for a flicker of black along the parapet, just above the roofs. A flicker of black, edged in crimson, that seemed to flutter out from behind the near turret.

And then, in an instant, the black was gone.

Seven

On any other day, Flan would have enjoyed the mazelike journey to the old marketplace beneath Blakely Manor. On the rare occasions that Uncle allowed her the freedom to go out unaccompanied, she loved to explore the city. Each time she went out, she chose a different route, seeking secluded side streets, hidden alleys, and out-of-the-way passageways she'd never run across before. Flan had searched the city that way her whole life, trying to find some clue that would explain who she was or where she came from.

But on that day, her mind was too full. Had she truly seen someone atop the manor? And more particularly, had he—or she—seen Flan? She wasn't sure what rules governed the shaving of willow tree bark, but if a long-lost Blakely had indeed returned to clear the grounds and reclaim the ancient family home, they would most certainly not be pleased to find a town girl slipping through their fence and tromping up the banks of their stream uninvited.

Bother. Between tumbling on her backside behind the tavern, fending off kisses from an unknown young man in the alleyway, and spying a stranger atop a manor house that was supposed to be abandoned, she had already wasted precious time. And all the while, her uncle waited at home, depending on her quick return, enduring who knew what sort of agony. She picked up her skirts and hurried along the cobblestone lane.

The air was damp, the afternoon chilled. The sun was but a distant memory, hidden behind a bank of iron gray clouds that cloaked the rooftops. Its rays could not hope to break through the blackness of the cramped alleyway. As Flan wound her way closer and closer to the address carefully penned on the parchment, the alleys became narrower and more twisted, passageways branching off in every direction, until Flan felt as if she were trapped in a rabbit warren and wondered if she should leave a trail of bread crumbs to find her way out.

At one time the various alleyways had sported wooden street signs, displaying their names, but most of the signs were now missing or broken. She peered at them, and pieced together a few street names: Potter Court and Bobbin Lane.

Likewise, the brightly colored signs that had once proudly displayed the names of stores and workshops were faded in memory and time. Most were so faint Flan could not hope to read them, but she puzzled out *T'S FIN APESTRIES* as someone's fine tapestries. Another shop was painted with an *E*, or perhaps it was an *F*. The middle of the sign was so splintered and faded, she could only make out the last three faint letters: *ACE*. She frowned. ACE? Some sort of laceworks, perhaps. Which made sense, for she was now in the heart of the old textiles market. She'd heard Uncle talk about the silks and needlepoint and other finery the marketplace had been known for in its heyday, before it, like the manor house on the hill beyond, had fallen into ruin.

Flan hurried past the laceworks and rounded a corner. She stopped and squinted in the dim light, studying the parchment, then scanning the alley walls. Finally. She had found what she was looking for, or at least, what she hoped she was looking for. She tucked the parchment back into the pocket of her cloak and scrambled across the wet stone, into the shadow of an enormous arched entryway, built into the sooty brick.

Flan was not a small person, but even she felt dwarfed as she made her way to the recessed doorway. She tucked the list into her empty string bag and gave three sharp raps on the door with the rusted iron door knocker.

She waited.

And waited.

And waited some more.

Uncle had said it would take some time, that she should be patient. That she should not knock again. That she should simply wait.

The warped wooden door was divided into two parts, top and bottom, ancient paint peeling equally from both halves. She pulled her cloak around her to stave off the chill as she stared at it, willing it to open. Open and allow her to finish this unpleasant business so that she could get back to Uncle.

At long last she heard the clatter of a bolt being pulled back, a latch clicking free. The top half of the door groaned open.

Flan braced herself. She had no idea what to expect. She only knew Uncle had warned her not to appear startled. She pasted a smile on her face.

And at first she saw nothing but the yawning black opening where the top of the door had been. Then she started as two shiny dark eyes peered out.

The creature leaned down, and Flan saw that she was a troll, her face broad, her nose long and twisted to the side, her skin mottled and rough, nearly reptilian in both texture and color. The woman's chin disappeared into the lumpy skin of her neck, and her shoulders hunched forward, one pitched higher than the other. She was more unsettling than the troll masks Flan had seen in shop windows before All Hallows' Eve, and her face appeared even the more hideous against the ruffled collar of her elegant and finely made green silk gown, the long red hair that curled over her shoulder in the most fashionable style, and the dazzling ruby earrings that sparkled in ears that flopped low along her face.

"Moonstones in your shoe." The woman snorted, blasting out the stench of rotting meat and decayed cabbage, her breath so putrid it nearly knocked Flan backward into the alley. "Won't protect you. Lily-livered amulet in the first place, and it doesn't work on trolls anyway, you know. We see everything."

"Oh. Of course." Flan realized she had been staring at the troll for longer than was polite. She swallowed. "Madame LaGrange?"

The troll narrowed her eyes. Her mouth hardened into a gash. "If you don't know to whom you speak, you clearly have no business here." She slapped the door with one gnarled palm, swinging it closed.

"No!" Flan thrust her hand up onto the door's ledge, knuckles throbbing, her hand crushed so tightly in the door, she feared her bones would snap.

"I apologize if I've offended you," she managed to utter through gritted teeth. "I've never been in this part of the city before, and I was afraid I'd lost my way."

She rested her head against the grimy brick. Madame LaGrange had not gone far. Flan could hear her snorting behind the door, could still smell the stench of her breath.

She tried again. "My uncle warned me to use my best manners, to show you the utmost respect. I believe you know him—Monsieur Anatole? He owns Monsieur Anatole's Books, Wonders, and Charms in Wicker Street, and he sorely needs some black powder. Please don't punish him for my rude behavior."

The snorting stopped, and for a moment Flan feared Madame LaGrange had gone for good, leaving her hand stuck fast in the doorway.

"You're a liar." Madame LaGrange's bark was muffled by the door. "Anatole has no family. Not here."

"No. I mean, yes. You're right." Flan tried to keep the panic from her voice. "He has no blood family. But he does have me. He adopted me as a baby and raised me as if I were his blood. Truly. I would not lie about that."

Madame LaGrange hissed. "Adopted? You take me for

a fool if you think I'll swallow that story. What is your name, you so-called adopted niece of Anatole?"

"Flan," she said. "Flannery Lane."

Again the snorting stopped. Flan listened.

Finally the door squeaked open, no more than a crack.

But enough for Flan to pull her hand free. She clasped and unclasped her fingers, trying to wriggle the blaze of pain from her knuckles.

The dark eyes peered out once more. "Flannery Lane?" She paused. "Are you sure?"

"Of course I'm sure." Flan looked at her. "It's *my* name, isn't it?"

Madame LaGrange shrugged one lopsided shoulder. "Maybe yes, maybe no. Still. That tells me much."

Flan stopped. Her heart thumped in her chest. "Tells you what? Something of my family? Something of my past?"

The troll's face hardened. "You expect Madame LaGrange to share her gifts for nothing? You want to know what I know about you, Flannery Lane, you give me something in return."

"Give?" Flan stared at her. "But I have nothing you—no, wait! I do. I can pay you."

With one trembling hand she held up the gold coin Uncle had given her.

"Pfft." Madame LaGrange narrowed her eyes. "Only one? One gold coin buys missy exactly one thing—either what you want to know or what Anatole wants you to bring to him. You want both? You pay for both."

Pay. Pay. She had to pay. Flan ran frantic hands through her cloak pockets, and came up empty, as she'd known she would. Uncle never allowed her out with more than she would need. He said he feared she would be pickpocketed, but she suspected his true fear was something more—that she would catch a thief with his hand in her pocket and use her magic to stop him.

"Madame LaGrange, please."

A whisper of a thought crossed Flan's mind. She could give up the black powder—powder Uncle himself had sworn he would never allow into his shop again—for a clue to her past.

Flan closed her eyes. No. Uncle was depending on her, and she could not betray him.

"I haven't got but the one gold coin." She braced her hands against the doorframe so that the troll could not shut her out. She did not like to ask anything of anyone. But she had no choice now but to beg. "If you know something of where I come from, I must know it. I'll find a way to repay your—your kindness. *Please.*"

"Kindness? Is that what you take me for? *Kind?*" Madame LaGrange snorted and slapped at the door as if to slam it shut again.

Flan caught the door, this time not allowing her fingers to become mashed in the doorway.

"Fine," she said. "Just the black powder then."

Madame LaGrange nodded, apparently satisfied. She banged the door shut so abruptly and with such force that Flan jumped back, bumping her head on the doorway brick and, to her shame, letting out a small squeal. She slid a mittened hand under her hood to rub the sore spot on her head while still flexing the pain from her knuckles.

After a time, Madame LaGrange returned, this time holding a thick twist of paper.

"I believe this is what the young missy has come for." The troll smiled, showing blackened and twisted teeth.

She held out the paper, and for a moment, Flan was afraid to reach for it, afraid of what further pain this visit could inflict on her. At last she plucked the paper from the troll's hand. Holding it close, she worked one end loose, just a bit, the way Uncle had instructed her.

She peered into the twist of paper. The granules inside certainly *looked* like black powder. She sniffed. The sharp scent pricked her nose. It certainly *smelled* like black powder.

Flan nodded and held out the gold coin. Madame LaGrange snapped it from her palm and ran a clawed fingernail across its surface.

"Thank you, young *Flan*." Madame LaGrange looked up. She stared at Flan for a long while. "I like you, Flannery Lane. You remind me very much of someone I once knew. So I will tell you this, no charge. You're close. You're very close."

"Close?" Flan frowned. "To what?"

But Madame LaGrange didn't answer. She swung the door shut without a word. The latch clicked, and the bolt clanked home.

Eight

"Uncle?" Flan clattered up the steps and pushed open the door. "Uncle, I'm back. I have what you need."

She clicked the door shut behind her and shrugged off her cloak. An icy nip hung in the room. Uncle's steam-heat system must have burned low. She rubbed her hands together and headed into the parlor, thinking to warm herself before the fire. She'd had enough of sudden chills for one day.

Obsidian curled himself around her legs. Merlin snuffled and poked his head out from behind the umbrella stand. But of her uncle, she saw nothing. The parlor was empty, the hearth grown cold.

She checked Uncle's bedchamber and the kitchen—and did not find him.

"Uncle?" She pushed down the panic that had risen in her throat.

She slid open the purple velvet curtain that separated the parlor from Anatole's workroom. She found him slumped over his grimoire at the table. His writing instruments and jars of spell components—dragon scales, dried holly, tincture of gryphon's breath—lay scattered on the table around him.

"Uncle?"

His eyes fluttered open. "Flan." His voice was no more than a wheeze. "You're home." With trembling hands, he pushed himself up. His spectacles, the frames bent, fell from his nose.

"You've been working." Flan pressed her palm to his forehead. His skin felt clammy and cold.

He batted her hand away. "You gathered the spell components?" he croaked.

Flan set her string bag on the table before him. "You could have warned me she was a troll. I braced myself and somehow managed not to flinch." She held her hand over the heat stove. Stone cold. She screeched the door open. "But some sort of hint would have been helpful."

Anatole gave her a weak smile. "So you had no trouble."

Flan stoked the embers with the poker. "None."

She slid a log into the stove, swung the door shut, and latched it. She did not feel it necessary to mention the odd way Madame LaGrange had reacted to her name, nor the fact that she had told the troll her name at all. Flan flexed her hand. Her knuckles still ached from the crushing encounter with Madame LaGrange's doorway.

Likewise she did not tell him of the stranger behind the tavern or the flick of black along the parapets of Blakely Manor. She wanted her uncle to recover, not spend his remaining strength fretting over her.

"I have what you need." Flan pulled the willow bark and black powder from her string bag. "But do you think it wise—"

Anatole held up his hand. "Save your breath. I can do it." He straightened the frames of his spectacles as well as he could, settled them onto his nose and paged through the grimoire until he found the potion: *Protectus Maximus*.

"I'll just need to fetch my alembic and I can begin." He pushed himself up, straightened his robes, and headed for the cabinet which held his alchemy supplies. "Go back down to the shop. I don't need your help." Anatole gathered the alembic and a mortar and pestle and carried them to his work table. He ground the willow bark with his mortar and pestle and dropped the dust into the glass vessel.

"But Uncle—"

"Flan, leave me be." Anatole spoke without turning around. He poured a small portion of black powder in the bowl. "Don't you have some dusting to do?"

"Yes." Flan snorted. "It seems I always have dusting to do."

She turned on the heel of her boot and marched through the curtain and down to the bookshop.

As she dusted, she heard her uncle intone the magic runes. "*YOU-et.*" The magic crackled even in the staircase. "*VEE-ex. CUE-dot.*"

And then she heard a thump.

"Uncle?"

She thundered back up the stairs and found her uncle slumped over his work table, the beaker half filled with potion, his hands clasped over his throat.

"Uncle!"

Flan raced to his side. She slid her arms around him to keep him from falling to the floor. His breath rattled in his chest. His entire body trembled.

"Flan." His voice was no more than a wheeze. "The potion. The black powder—"

"Shhh. I know." She tried to steady him, tried to steady the panic that rose in her throat like bile. "Don't try to speak."

Flan helped her uncle from the workshop and into his bedchamber, using his great oaken wand as a cane. She settled him in his bed as best she could, slid his boots from his feet, pulled his spectacles from his nose, and placed them on the bedside table.

He grasped at her arm with trembling fingers. "Flan, promise me—" His voice crumbled into a breathless croak.

"Yes, I will take care of the shop. You know you never need worry about that." She tucked his quilts around his chin. "You only need worry about resting, and feeling better."

"No." He looked up at her, his eyes burning with fever. "You must promise—"

He coughed so hard Flan feared he might not take another breath. She propped a pillow under his head and rubbed his back to coax the cough free.

"Magic . . . has brought nothing . . . but suffering," he rasped. "You can't—you must promise. When I'm gone—"

"Uncle." Panic rose in her chest, and she did her best to push it back down. "You're—"

"No magic. Swear to me, Flan. *Swear to me.*"

"Yes. Fine. I swear." She brushed his hair from his fevered cheeks. "Now swear to *me* that you will rest."

But Uncle did not answer. He had already slumped into his pillows, asleep.

Flan settled into the chair beside his bed, Obsidian clasped tight in her arms.

Nine

Early the next morning, before the sun had even attempted to pierce the fog, a sudden pounding on the bookshop door sent Flan scrambling from her chair.

"Anatole? Monsieur Anatole!" A woman's voice rang out. It was followed by a man's. "Anatole. You in there?"

Flan pulled her bed jacket around her, lit the bedside lamp, and peeked at her uncle.

He slumbered fitfully, his skin gray and pale in the lamplight, with mere hollows where his usually ruddy cheeks should have been.

"Uncle?" Flan gently shook him. But he did not awake. His hands twitched, and his breath rattled in his chest. On the pillow beside him, Merlin snuffled and quivered, as if he, too, rested only in fits and starts.

The pounding sounded again.

"Anatole!" It was the butcher. Flan recognized his voice. "We need your help!"

Flan's heart thudded. Uncle was in no state to answer the door. He was in no state to help anyone, including himself. But she could not possibly allow the butcher and his wife—or anyone, for that matter—to see Uncle right now. They would think him more bungling than ever. Or worse, they would guess he'd been cursed. Either way, he would not be able to help them, and they would waste little time spreading the news to all of Wicker Street.

She scooped Obsidian into her arms, scuffed downstairs, and threaded her way through the bookshop. The butcher and his wife stood outside, at the bottom of the steps, like two plump quivering sausages, the dense Wicker Street fog nearly swallowing them whole.

Flan settled Obsidian on the window ledge and unlatched the door, and the two of them practically fell into the shop. They were out of breath, their faces flushed. Mrs. MacDougal's cloak was twisted round her, as if she'd thrown it on in the dark as she and her husband scurried to the shop. The butcher hadn't taken time to don a cloak at all.

He wiped a meaty hand across his forehead. "The amulet didn't work. Should have known better than to put my trust in that so-called wizard."

"Didn't work?" Flan blinked. She'd given the butcher and his brownies little thought since he'd left the parlor with the copper-wrapped amulet—and her uncle had collapsed. "What do you mean it didn't work?"

The butcher glared at Flan. "I mean it's gotten worse. I hung the amulet, just like he told me. And this morning when I came down to open up shop, I found the door open."

"Not just open," said his wife. "Hanging by a single bolt. They'd practically ripped it from its very hinges."

"Oh, my." Flan frowned. Brownies could be destructive, it was true, but on a much smaller scale—a broken plate, a disheveled drawer, a sack of sugar split open and spilled to the floor. She'd never heard of a brownie big enough or strong enough to rip a door from its hinges.

"But that's not the half of it." Mrs. MacDougal drew in a breath, and Flan saw a tear brimming over her stout cheek. Her chin quivered. "Miss Nibbles has gone missing. I've looked all morning and can't find a sign of her. I couldn't even lure her back with a dish of her favorite sardines. It's like she vanished into thin air."

"Slipped out the door." The butcher glared at Flan. "And why wouldn't she? It was wide open, swinging in the fog. And your uncle's amulet still hanging there, too, not disturbed one whit." He held up the plain metal amulet with the copper strand. "Completely useless."

As Flan took the amulet, a gust of chill morning air swept through the shop, flickering the flame of the lamp in her hand and fluttering the pages of the open books on display in the window. Flan realized she was still holding the door open.

"Where are my manners?" she said. "Here. Come in where it's warm."

She ushered the butcher and his wife into the shop. She could not send them away with their problem unsolved, complaining loudly to anyone who would listen that Monsieur Anatole had failed them.

She rubbed a hand over her face. Uncle always seemed so calm, so assured, when a frantic client pounded at the door, as if he knew precisely what to do.

But the butcher and his wife were waiting, and Flan had no idea what to do.

Tea. The word dropped into her mind out of nowhere. Flan blinked. Tea. Of course.

"Excuse me, I'll be right back." She gave the butcher and his wife her calmest, most reassuring smile, settled them into a pair of cushy high-backed chairs at the end of the work counter, and bounded up the staircase, Obsidian in her arms.

She peeked in on Uncle. He still looked feverish. But at least the rattling in his chest had quieted. Merlin, too, seemed to be resting more easily.

She took a deep breath. She would have to take care of this herself. Uncle wouldn't like it, but once he was well again, he would understand. At least, she hoped he would understand. For what other choice did she have?

Flan slipped into the kitchen, where she worked quickly, spelling the cooled tea kettle to quickly reheat the water, flicking her hazel wood wand to pull cups, saucers, spoons, and a tin of biscuits from the cupboard, enchanting the milk bottle to pour a small pitcher of milk. It was magic, yes, which she'd promised not to use, but surely Uncle could not object. It was only a bit of kitchen magic, after all—barely magic at all.

She clinked the tea things onto a tray, then bounded back downstairs again, Obsidian at her feet.

"Here we are." Flan set the tray on the counter beside the oil lamp, brushed a wayward strand of hair from her face, and began to pour the steaming tea.

"Uh, begging your pardon." The butcher glanced behind her, toward the stairs. "Your uncle. Is he coming down?"

"Yes, well, you see." As Flan gathered her thoughts, she set a cup of tea in front of the butcher and moved the pitcher of milk within his reach. "Uncle is . . . working. On a stronger protection spell." She gave the butcher a grave but encouraging look. "He sensed that your brownie troubles might be a bit thornier than the average."

Mrs. MacDougal nodded and poked her husband in the chest. "You see? I told you he'd know what to do."

But Master MacDougal knotted his forehead into a puzzled frown. "So . . . he's *not* coming?"

"He wants to." Flan set a cup of tea in front of his wife. "You know he wants nothing more than to help his neighbors and friends. He hates not being here for you. But he's rather at the tricky part of the spell at the moment. If he stops now, before it's finished, well, I shudder to think what might happen. You understand, I'm sure."

The MacDougals nodded, but narrowed their eyes—suspiciously, it seemed to Flan.

"He's asked me to help him," she said quickly. "Help him to help you. So." Flan poured herself a cup of tea. She settled onto a tall stool at the work counter and gave her tea a stir. Scrying, she told herself, did not count as magic. It was simply a matter of paying attention. "What sort of mischief did you find *inside* the shop?"

She peered at the froth in her cup. It swirled and, just as before, curled into the shape of a droplet.

A droplet. Flan shook her head. She blew into the steam.

"That's the funny thing," the butcher was saying. "There wasn't no mischief at all inside. Not the kind you mean.

Nothing broken. Nothing missing. Not even me best roast, which is what I would've taken if it was me. Things sure were disturbed, though, I can tell you."

His wife nodded. "Cleaned up. Just like before. Knives sparkling clean and lined up on the board. Blood all swabbed up. Tables cleared. The whole place even smelled better, sort of sweet like. Not at all like the dreadful stinking mess he usually leaves." She jerked a thumb at her husband. "If it weren't for the door pulled right off its frame, I wouldn't mind having someone else washing up for a change."

Flan glanced at her tea. The froth had drawn itself into the shape of wings. Bat wings. She stared at them. A bat? But the butcher's intruder could not be a bat. Could it? It would certainly explain how the intruder could get in and out of the shop at will, without being seen. A bat could simply flitter down the chimney flue. But it would not explain the sparkling knives or the floor swabbed clean. As far as she knew, bats had no special talent for scrubbing and mopping. And in any case, Flan had seen the butcher's. She knew the sort of mess the butcher made of things. Why, the intruder would find—

Flan froze. The intruder would find blood. Pools and splatters and *droplets* of blood. She sat very still for a moment. She could think of a creature, a very batlike creature, that would be most interested in blood.

She stared at the froth in her cup, the bat wings now swirling into spikes that looked almost like teeth. She shuddered.

"Miss Flan?"

Flan looked up. The butcher and his wife were watching her.

"Are you all right then?" said the butcher's wife. "You look a mite pale."

Flan swallowed. "Yes. I was simply—I need to give Uncle this information. He will know exactly what to do. Please make yourselves comfortable." She opened the tin of biscuits she'd set on the tray. "This will only take a moment."

She pushed the biscuits toward the MacDougals and bounded upstairs once more, Obsidian padding along behind.

When she reached Uncle's workshop, she pulled a book from his shelves. She blew the dust from its spine. It had been years since anyone had needed to consult its pages.

Obsidian gave a low hiss.

"Yes, Obsidian, it's *A Practical Guide to Vampires.*" Flan ran her hand over the cover. "Let us hope it does give me practical guidance."

She leafed through the book to find the pages she needed, then began pulling components from Uncle's shelves. She had promised—no, *sworn*—she wouldn't do magic. And she would not. But the MacDougals needed her, and not simply to keep them from whispering about Uncle behind his back. They had a problem, a deadly problem, and she was the only one who could help. She ran her finger down the page. None of these counters against vampires needed to be magically spelled. She would simply give them practical protections from this practical guide.

The tick of the grandfather clock echoed through the workshop. An early morning rain began tapping against the high dusty windows. Flan worked quickly and methodically to collect the items the butcher and his wife would need.

Then she bounded back downstairs, a small, smoke-filled vial in one hand. An amulet dangled from her wrist, its cluster of small silver bells jingling as she thumped down the steps.

She found Mrs. MacDougal nibbling absently on her biscuit. Her husband crumbled his, bit by bit, in his beefy hands. They both looked up expectantly as she crossed to the counter.

Flan held up the vial. "Burned ash of the alder tree. Scatter it along doorways, windowsills, and any other entry point into your butcher shop. Do not forget the fireplace. Troublesome beings can easily slip unnoticed down a chimney." She did not mention that the troublesome beings in this case were plainly not household brownies. She handed the vial to the butcher. "Careful. It's still quite warm."

The butcher nodded and slid the vial into a pocket of his apron.

"Hang this"—She held up the amulet of bells—"in the center of your shop, in a spot where it will catch a breeze."

The butcher nodded again and took the bells. They jangled in his meaty fist. "Begging your pardon, but couldn't we hang them in a far corner where the breeze never blows instead? I hate to think of 'em tinkling like that all day."

"I'm afraid not," said Flan. "They would hardly ward off evil if they're silent."

The butcher's wife looked askance at the bells. "I think I'd almost rather have intruders. A thing like that could drive a person buggy."

"Yes." Flan considered the bells. "Keep them under wraps during the day then, but be sure to hang them when you close up for the evening. Does hawthorn grow near your shop?"

The butcher and his wife looked at each other.

"Hawthorn? No," said the butcher. "None that I can recollect."

"Do you have garlic then?"

"Garlic?" The butcher frowned. "Why it almost sounds like you think a—"

Flan waved a hand. "It matters little what I think. I'm simply conveying Uncle Anatole's instructions."

After all, it would do little good to frighten the man witless. Or allow him—and all of Wicker Street—to think a vampire had slipped into the city under Monsieur Anatole's very nose, and him none the wiser.

She stopped. Under his very nose. That's precisely what had happened. But Uncle's nose had scarcely been working properly while this vampire went about his business, had it?

"Miss Flan?"

"Uh . . . yes." She shook her head and turned to the butcher's wife. "A woman as lovely as you, Mrs. MacDougal, must have a mirror at hand. Place it just inside the shop door at night, and make sure it is well illuminated by lamplight."

The butcher's wife frowned. "And this mirror will ward off brownies."

"A mirror can ward off all manner of difficulties. You would be surprised."

"And as for your cat, I've asked Uncle to cast a location spell for breathing beings. If she is—" Flan swallowed. She dare not mention what fate a vampire may have in mind for Miss Nibbles. "If she is still in the city, Miss Nibbles should be home soon."

She would have warned the butcher and his wife not to invite strangers into their shop, for a vampire could not enter a place unless he—or she—were invited. But of course it was too late for that. They must have, unaware, already allowed this vampire in at some point. And once he had been invited, he could forever more enter at will.

Instead, Flan ushered the MacDougals from the book-shop, loaded down with amulets, protections, and instructions. She only hoped that what she'd given them would be enough.

She clicked the lock into place behind them, then turned to the rows and rows of books. If a vampire were stalking the butcher's shop, he—or she—wanted but one thing: blood. But blood from the butcher's would not sustain the vampire for long, and soon he would be hunting other victims, victims more appealing than the butcher's cat.

And Flan was convinced he'd already chosen his first— Uncle Anatole.

She shuddered. She did not like to think it, but *some-body* had cursed her uncle, and if a vampire had targeted Wicker Street, his task would become much easier if he first destroyed the resident wizard's protection magic. For while Wicker Street may not believe in Anatole's magic, Flan knew how truly powerful it could be. And so, it seemed, did this vampire.

After careful study, she selected a few volumes and blew the dust off the covers. She paged through the first book till she found the spell she was looking for, then pulled the hazel wood wand from her pocket.

Obsidian cast a wary look at the wand.

"I know," Flan told him. "But their cat is missing. If you were missing, would you have me sit idly by and not do everything in my power to find you? I've chosen a location spell that uses only the tamest of magic, the sort of magic many a Wicker Street wife could summon up."

The cat yawned and curled into one of the plush high-backed chairs.

Flan cast the location spell for living things, then slid the wand back into her pocket and settled down at the counter with the remaining books and a fresh cup of tea.

She felt a sudden need to read about the undead.

Ten

ong after the clock tower had struck midnight, Flan started awake. She glanced over at Uncle. He seemed to be sleeping restfully. She could see the regular rise and fall of his chest.

But something had awakened her. She sat up in the bedside chair, rubbed at the cramp in her neck, and pulled Obsidian close.

"Did you hear something?" she whispered.

The cat yawned.

Flan sat very still.

"There it is again."

She heard it quite distinctly this time—an insistent rapping on the bookshop door.

"Bother." She tightened her bed jacket around her. "Can no one think to visit the shop when we're actually open?"

She clambered downstairs holding Obsidian snug beneath her chin, her lamp painting distorted shadows above them on the staircase wall. She threaded her way through the shop and peered through the front window.

A young man stood outside the door, at the bottom of the steps. His back was to her, the collar of his topcoat pulled up to ward off the damp and the chill.

She clicked the latch and pulled the door open just a crack.

"May I help you?" she asked.

The young man turned—

—and Flan caught her breath.

It was the young man from the alley, the stranger with the black hair.

He pulled his top hat from his head and held it to his chest in fine gentlemanly fashion. "This is Monsieur Anatole's Books, Wonders, and Charms, I believe. You are the proprietor?"

He peered through the crack of the door. His pale eyes met hers, and once again all words flew from her head.

Flan, momentarily stunned, found herself saying, "Yes."

The young man offered a hesitant smile. "I need a bit of help of an urgent and rather delicate nature, and I've been told this is where I should come." He cast a glance over his shoulder. "Would it be possible for me to come in? I could explain the matter in greater detail."

He gave her such an honestly pleading look that her first instinct was to fling the door wide open.

But, she reminded herself, he was a complete stranger.

As if reading her mind, he said, "I understand your hesitation. You see"—he lowered his voice—"I've come for a talisman. A very specific kind of talisman. I've come for a Talisman of Undead Mastery."

Flan nearly dropped her lamp. A Talisman of Undead Mastery? She'd just been reading of that. This fellow, this stranger, sought protection from—and a weapon against—vampires. A powerful weapon, prized by vampire hunters in every land.

She studied the young man. His fine-chiseled features lit up as he spoke, his voice filled with sincerity and passion, his broad shoulders moved easily beneath the fine lines of his topcoat.

Yes, she could most definitely see him as a vampire hunter. He leaned toward her, better to see through the crack of the door, and the spicy clean scent that drifted into the shop made Flan a bit dizzy. Before she knew what she was doing, she had opened the door and gestured for the young man to enter.

"Thank you." He hesitated a moment, then slipped quickly through the door. He stopped short when he had full view of Flan. "It's you. I mean—forgive me. Where are my manners?" He gave a small bow. "It's lovely to see you again."

Obsidian let out a low murmur, deep in his throat, half growl, half purr. Flan, to her great horror, felt a burn creep up her neck to her face. She held a hand to her cheek. She knew she must be blushing, and there was nothing she could do to stop it.

She tipped her head. "Good to see you too." She was horrified to hear her voice float across the shop, as high-pitched and twittering as Mistress Dobbins, the dressmaker.

She set Obsidian on a shelf and scrambled to clear the stacks of books from the counter.

She led the stranger to the two stools at the work counter, and as she began to climb upon one, he reached to pull it out for her. She found herself rather tangled in his arms, her chin bumping him squarely in the forehead.

"Oh! I—are you all right? I'm—I'm sorry." She flailed a bit, disentangling herself from his arms and coattails, not knowing quite what to do with her hands.

The young man stepped back, blinking, clearly startled from the blow. "No, it is I who should apologize." As he rubbed his bumped forehead, a smile tugged at the corners of his mouth. "I'd forgotten how self-sufficient you are. You clearly like gentlemen pulling your chair out for you even less than you like them rescuing you from alleyway rubble."

Again Flan felt the red burn creep up her cheeks. "No! I just—" She took a breath. "I'm used to taking care of myself."

The young man studied her, his face more serious now. He nodded. "I've had to do more than a small bit of that myself."

He perched upon the other stool, one long leg reaching the floor, the other dangling, sure and graceful. He set his black silk top hat beside him on the counter and rested an elbow on the counter's edge, with the easy confidence of one who has never known anything but the highest station in life.

Obsidian leaped from the bookshelf and circled him, warily weaving beneath the legs of the counter.

The young man gave Flan an expectant look, and with a start, she remembered he thought her the proprietor. Crone's nightgown! What was wrong with her? She had led this fellow to believe that *she* was the great wizard of the shop.

And against her will, a tingle of excitement prickled her spine. She *could* be the wizard of the shop. She had helped the butcher and his wife, after all, and they had been none the wiser. She had promised she would do no magic, but if a vampire truly was behind Uncle's curse, she would need to use everything she knew—including magic—to save him. She was loath to depend on a vampire hunter to help her, but she could certainly help the vampire hunter.

She settled onto her stool. "A Talisman of Undead Mastery. Interesting request."

The young man nodded. "I'm prepared to pay, no matter the cost. You see, it must be crafted of ruby and silver. Nothing less will do."

He began describing the sort of talisman he required, gesturing with his hands to give her a clearer picture, and Flan had to force herself to stop staring at his graceful fingers long enough to allow his words to seep into her brain.

"I need a way to carry it with me without attracting attention, perhaps in a small case," he said.

"I could fashion a small velvet pouch, elegant and dark, with drawstrings to keep the amulet at hand."

"No. Oh . . . no. I will definitely need a case. Some sort of metal case. Lead perhaps."

Flan frowned. "Lead?"

The stranger nodded. "To give it . . . heft."

"Lead would certainly give it that."

"And tightly sealed." The young man spoke in earnest. "Is that possible?"

Flan spread her arms wide, as she knew Anatole would do. "Anything is possible," she said, which was what her uncle used to always say, back when the shop did brisk business.

The stranger smiled in relief. "That's settled then. When should I return?"

Flan considered this. She had never created a talisman on her own before, but she was certain she could complete it in a single afternoon, if she had the right components. But first she needed to collect the components, and then there was the matter of the case. That would take some doing. And if anything went wrong, she would need to correct it.

"Give me two days," she said. "That will be time enough."

"Two days." The stranger rose and bowed his head at Flan. "Adieu until then."

His pale gray eyes met hers once more, all but stopping the beat of her heart.

It was only after she'd watched his finely fitting topcoat vanish into the fog that Flan realized she had forgotten to ask his name.

Eleven

Early the next morning, Flan slipped from the bookshop, rattled the door shut behind her, and made sure the lock clicked home. She tucked her list into her mitten. She had much to do and little time to do it. The thrill of it—and also the panic—nearly burst from her chest.

The sun was just beginning to burn off the nighttime fog, but a mist still shrouded the street. She would stop by the baker's first, while the pastries were fresh. She clattered up the three stone steps to the walkway—

—and ran headlong into a throng of shopkeepers chattering outside the bookshop's very windows. Old Mrs. Loveworthy was bent in earnest conversation with Mistress Dobbins, the dressmaker from Threadneedle Alley.

"No one knows when he arrived," Mrs. Loveworthy was saying. "But he must have brought with him a considerable household staff."

"Oh, yes." Mistress Dobbins nodded, her cap bobbing against her forehead. "A *considerable* staff."

Flan frowned. Someone newly arrived? With a household

85

staff? Her mind darted to the black-haired stranger. Could he be the one they were prattling on about?

Flan folded her fingers around the list in her mitten and slipped past, giving a nod to Mrs. Loveworthy and Mistress Dobbins. She almost wished she could stop by the dressmaker's shop, where Gwen was apprenticed. Gwen—or at least, the Gwen of old—would have helped her sort out a way to help Uncle, would have clamored to hear every detail of the black-haired stranger.

A twinge of sorrow tugged at Flan, the way it always did when she thought of Gwen.

She bent her head against the cold and hurried on, only to catch another snippet of conversation as she passed a flock of Wicker Street women huddled outside the butcher's.

"I've heard he's using the family coat of arms," said Mrs. Lindstrom, Gwen's mother. "Do you think he's brought a wife?"

"I've seen no female frills about the estate," said Mrs. Childers, who kept the inn at the end of the lane. "The kitchen garden has been torn out altogether, and all its lovely herbs with it. But I can't imagine someone of that station arriving without a wife."

A wife? Could the stranger truly have a wife? A pang of jealousy stabbed Flan's chest.

Which was utterly ridiculous. She shook her head. The stranger was simply someone who had stopped by the shop to make a purchase, just as he had probably stopped by the butcher's or the baker's or the haberdasher's. She had no claim to him.

As the women chattered on, the butcher's wife burst from her shop, out of breath, one stout hand pressed to her even stouter bosom. For a moment, Flan froze. She feared the butcher's nighttime intruder had struck again.

But Mrs. MacDougal had something else entirely on her mind.

"He is," she gasped. "It's just as we suspected. I've found out his name."

"His name!" A twitter of delight swept through the crowd.

The butcher's wife nodded. "He's a Blakely, all right. A Master *Adrian* Blakely, the eighth Viscount Blakely. I've not yet determined where he's come from. But I will, mind you." She shook a stout finger. "I will."

A Blakely. Flan realized she had stopped dead in her tracks and was now blatantly eavesdropping. She picked up her step, hurrying toward the baker's once more.

But a Blakely. A Master Adrian Blakely, eighth Viscount Blakely. It was just as she had suspected. He was the new viscount arrived to claim the great manor. He was the one who had cleared the brambles. He was the one who had trimmed the lawns. He was the one she'd seen atop the manor's parapet—the one she feared had seen her.

But he had come seeking a Talisman of Undead Mastery. It was as she thought—he *was* a vampire hunter, just like his ancestors.

"It's been far too long since we've had a Blakely in our midst," Mrs. MacDougal said.

"You can say that again," Mrs. Childers chimed in. "Now that there's a Blakely back in town, we'll be safe again."

It was then Flan realized that a large part of the excitement sweeping through Wicker Street was actually a highly charged sense of hope—and relief. The townspeople had been feeling vulnerable, in need of protection. No matter that Monsieur Anatole was right there, in their very midst, *offering* protection no matter how poorly they treated him.

And they had treated him poorly indeed. Flan shook her head. It had started the previous spring, on the night Gwen's father had come to Uncle in desperation. Things had been happening in his smithy, puzzling things, alarming things. An anvil had fallen on his foot. A vat of molten iron had tipped over on the forge. A shower of sparks had nearly caught a wagon on fire. The blacksmith was convinced the place had been cursed by fiends.

Uncle listened, and watched, in that keen-sighted way of his, and discerned that Master Lindstrom's trouble was not a plague of fiends. Master Lindstrom's trouble was his eyesight. Uncle fashioned the blacksmith a pair of spectacles and sent him on his way.

But Master Lindstrom was not used to wearing eyeglasses. He was not used to them sliding down the sweat of his nose. He was not used to them fogging up as he leaned over a blast of heat. He laid them aside, and when the accidents continued to plague his smithy, he paid another visit to Monsieur Anatole, again complaining of fiends.

He was not pleased when Anatole insisted he needed only a simple adjustment to his spectacles. Uncle had been experimenting with a potion, a most powerful protection that employed black powder as its main component, and when he turned away to tighten the earpieces on the spectacles, the blacksmith had pinched the potion from Uncle's work table.

The blacksmith returned to the smithy, sprinkled the potion around the doors and windows, then he fired up his forge and set to work, thinking himself quite clever to have taken the protection of his smithy into his own hands.

Oh, yes. Quite clever. Flan shook her head. The man had filled his shop with black powder, then stoked his fire to a roaring blaze. It was nothing short of a miracle that Master Lindstrom had survived the explosion.

With one arm shriveled, and one badly scarred leg dragging uselessly behind when he walked, Master Lindstrom could not hope to continue work as a blacksmith. Mrs. Lindstrom had resorted to taking in mending, and they had forbidden Gwen from spending time with Flan, or even speaking to her in the street.

Wicker Street blamed Anatole, and again Flan had been treated to no end of gossip:

"Lord Blakely knew how to handle *his* protection materials."

"Lord Blakely certainly never set a Wicker Street shop ablaze."

"If Lord Blakely were here, he would not have let this happen."

Lord Blakely! Flan kicked at a swirl of leaves on the walkway. She had grown bone weary of hearing about Lord Xander Blakely.

To the townsfolk, it was as if the soft underbelly of the city had been exposed these last months since the smithy fire, laid open to whatever evil might chance by.

And now, with the arrival of a new viscount, the people once again held hope that safety and security would once again blanket the city. Oh, yes. Flan kicked at a loose pebble. Simply get a Blakely back to town, and suddenly all your worries and fears would vanish.

Still, the Blakelys *had* always protected the city, most notably from vampires. If Flan were right, if a vampire had begun stalking Wicker Street, then she, too, should welcome the protection. She should consider herself fortunate, consider the city fortunate, be grateful that just when they needed protection from a vampire, a member of a great vampire-hunting family had arrived.

Grateful. She shook her head. The very idea of needing to feel grateful stood her hair on end. The Blakelys had never done anything for her, nor for her uncle, and likely never would. Which was just as well. She could take care of them both, as she always had.

Flan pulled her cloak close and quickened her pace. She would love to dawdle and gather more gossip, but she had errands to complete, beginning with the bakery. Uncle had eaten scarcely a morsel all day.

This curse had fixed its claws in him and would not let go. He would seem to rally, seem to regain enough strength to ask for a bit of broth and to send Flan down to the shop for stacks of books he could read as he recovered. Flan's heart would leap, thinking he had left the worst of it behind. But the next time she checked in on him, she would find him sprawled among the books in his bed, spectacles dented against his cheeks, broth only half finished, nearly out of his mind with fever. His face was wan, his shoulders drawn in weariness and pain. Even when he wasn't racked with fever, he could barely lift his head.

He needed something to keep up his strength, and Flan thought his favorite raspberry and cream mille-feuille might be the very thing.

As she pushed through the door of the bakery, a small bell jangled against the glass, and the heat from the baker's ovens wrapped her in a blanket of warmth. She stood just inside the door for a moment, breathing in the aroma of freshly baked bread.

She tossed her hood back and jostled her way through other customers. Half of Wicker Street, it seemed, had crowded into the tiny shop this morning. But they did not seem half as interested in the baker's goods as they were in Wicker Street gossip.

"Drawn by two perfectly matched black steeds, it was," said Mr. Jenks, the tavern keep, tapping his pipe. "The Blakelys always did have the best horses, they did. Late last night I went out to dump the dregs bucket, and suddenly there it was, like a bullet, racing out through the fog that always seems to cloak the manor gates, hooves thundering, wheels clattering, steam rising from the horses' backs. The moon had just slipped behind a bank of clouds, and between that and the fog, it was hard to see much more than a flash of black as he galloped past."

The butcher nodded. "I saw that very thing, this morning before the sun was even up. He come racing up the boulevard, back through the gates toward the manor, a streak of black glimmering through the fog."

A streak of black. Flan tapped a finger against her lip. Had the stranger arrived at the bookshop in a carriage pulled by two steaming black steeds? She hadn't seen a carriage, nor heard the clatter of wheels on the cobblestones. Still—

"Oh, I caught more than a streak of black, I did." Mistress Cornish, the milliner, nodded triumphantly, her several chins folding against her chest like an accordion. "I saw the viscount's face through the window of his coach."

"No!" The crowd murmured with excitement.

"Yes." The milliner's chins bobbed. "Handsome devil, he was—"

Oh, yes. Flan found herself nodding. Handsome. He was certainly that, with his dark hair falling over his eyes.

"—with his thicket of golden curls," the milliner continued.

Golden curls?

Mr. Jenks nodded. "I spied him pacing the mist-veiled parapet between the towers of the manor house. And a fine figure he cut. Tall and powerful and proud, a true lord of the manor."

Flan frowned. Her stranger was certainly tall, and he did cut a pleasing figure—at least, if one were the twittering sort of girl who looked for that sort of thing, which she, Flan, certainly was not. But he was slender, not powerfully built. He did seem confident, in a quiet sort of way, but proud? No, she could not describe him that way.

And he did not have golden curls.

She stopped. Her stranger was not Lord Blakely. She felt her heart slide to her stomach. She had convinced herself he must be the newly arrived viscount, and that she had been the first in Wicker Street to lay eyes on him. She'd been so certain. And now—he was not.

Crone's sake, Flan! She gave herself a shake. She *was* turning into a twittering sort of girl. So her stranger wasn't Lord Blakely. What difference did it make?

She paid for her sweets, then wormed her way through the crowd and out onto the walk beyond.

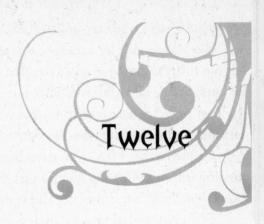

Twelve

Flan hurried along the cobblestones, head down against the wind, string bag clasped tight in her fist, paying little heed to the clusters of Wicker Street folk she passed on her way. So intent was she on returning to the bookshop that when she passed the alleyway, she did not notice the figure huddled in its black depths until a hand reached out and snatched at her cloak.

Flan whirled.

"Oh!" She clapped a hand over her mouth. "It's you."

"Shhh. If anyone sees us together, they'll run straight-away to my mother."

The figure pulled Flan into the alley, behind the jumble of barrels and crates heaped beside the back door of Mr. Jenks's White Mane Tavern, and for the first time in months, Flan found herself face to face with her dearest friend—or rather, her one-time dearest friend—Gwen. Huddled against the brick beside her stood Therese, the serving girl from Mrs. Childers's inn.

Behind them, the tavern door hung open a crack. They

stood in the pool of light that spilled out, the three of them, and at once it seemed so completely natural for them to be together—they had huddled together so very often as schoolgirls, Gwen and Flan especially—and at the same time so foreign, for neither Gwen nor Therese had spoken to her in the months since the blacksmith's fire.

Gwen and Therese cast looks at each other, as if they didn't know how to start and were too frightened even to begin.

Finally Gwen spoke. "We need your help. These past few days, someone has been following us. It happens either late at night when the sun has gone down, or in the morning before dawn, when the streets are foggy. At first it was just a movement." She rubbed a trembling hand over her face. "I'd catch a flutter or a flick out of the corner of my eye."

Therese nodded eagerly. "Same as me. But when I turned to see who was there, all I saw were shadows. I'd just give myself a shake and a good talking-to. 'Therese,' I'd say, 'it's just your mind playing tricks again.'"

"I thought that myself." Gwen nodded, her thick white-gold locks threatening to tumble out of the cap the dressmaker made her wear. "I tried to laugh it off, convince myself it was simply my own imagination run away with me again."

Her eyes met Flan's, and they both smiled, just a little. Flan knew how Gwen's imagination *could* run away with her, for it had run away with both of them so very often as they were growing up.

"But it's not my imagination if it's happening to both of us."

"And not to just us," said Therese. "To all the girls, all of us on Wicker Street."

"And in the lanes and alleys beyond," said Gwen. "We didn't say anything at first. It seemed silly to think evil could be lurking around every corner."

"But it's not silly." Therese shook her head vehemently. "I've been traveling Wicker Street my whole life, at all times of day and night. And I've never felt such a chill as this shadow that's been following me home of late."

Flan stared at them. "A shadow? And a chill? Are you sure?"

Therese nodded. "And the terrible flapping." She took a breath, as if to steady herself. "I heard it last night—the flapping, behind me, like bats, a whole swarm of them. A black shadow fell over me, and a kind of sweetness, this smell that sort of folded around me, like a veil, and that's when I felt the chill, straight down to my core like every bit of warmth was being sucked from my bones. The shadow grew closer and closer, and I knew for sure I was drawing my last breath. I swear the only thing that saved me was the music."

Flan frowned. "The music?"

Therese hesitated, but Gwen squeezed her arm in encouragement.

"Tell her, Therese," she said. "She'll tell Monsieur Anatole, and he'll know what to do."

Therese nodded. "It was a fancy sort of music. Sad and slow, like from a violin."

"A violin," Flan whispered. "Like Mrs. MacDougal's fiddle."

Therese frowned. "What?"

"Nothing." Flan shook her head. "Go on."

Therese nodded. "The music, it sort of floated through the air, and the shadow, well, it just stopped. Like the music had startled it. That's what it seemed like. And that's when I started running, my shoes pounding over the cobblestones, me screaming like my hair was on fire, and it could have been for all I know. I wouldn't have noticed. I just knew I had to get out of there, and I never would have, I swear, if it hadn't been for that music."

Gwen leaned forward, wisps of white-gold hair fluttered about her face. "Can you ask him to help us? Monsieur Anatole?"

Flan rubbed a hand over her forehead, trying to think what to do.

The vampire's thirsts seemed to be growing stronger. First leftover blood from the butcher's, then Uncle's curse, the cat, and now Wicker Street girls. She did not want to think what he would be driven to do next. She only knew she must find a way to stop him.

Gwen and Therese needed protection, powerful protection. And they needed it right away.

Flan laid a hand on Gwen's arm. "I'll speak to Uncle as soon as I get home. But for now—" She unbuckled her boots and shook the moonstones out of the toe. She'd been carrying them ever since Uncle had given them to her a few days ago. "Take these." She pressed a stone in each of their hands. "Uncle spelled them for me to ensure a safe journey. But you need them more than I."

97

Therese blinked at the smooth stone in her hand. "A bit of rock? I've got creeping evil following me, swooping down on great flapping wings, and all you can offer is a shiny pebble?"

"Just for now," said Flan. "I need to—I mean, Uncle needs to craft something more powerful, but it will take a small bit of time. Stay together, stay on the well-lighted parts of the street, and the stones should see you safely home. Come to the shop tomorrow and I will give you each a ring, fashioned from bone, to keep you safe."

Therese narrowed her eyes and studied Flan. She nodded. "Well. That's all right then."

Gwen clasped the moonstone in her palm. She gave Flan a smile. "Thank you," she said. "I knew you would help, I don't—I can't even—after everything—"

"I know." Flan nodded. "Come to the shop tomorrow."

Flan waited behind the crates as Gwen and Therese stole back out onto Wicker Street.

"What kind of wizard shop are they running anyway?" Therese's voice echoed back through the alley. "A stone, of all things. Cor blimey! I'd rather have the violin. If I couldn't play music, I could at least beat the creature off with it."

Thirteen

Uncle Anatole's face was pale, his fingers trembled, and when Flan gave his hand an encouraging squeeze, his cold palm felt damp with perspiration.

But when his gaze lit on the mille-feuille, he managed to struggle up on his bed pillows and take the plate from Flan's outstretched hand.

"Oh, my." He licked the cream icing from his fingers and closed his eyes in delight. "If this doesn't cure me, nothing will."

She tucked the blankets around him, set his tea on the bedside table, and squeezed his hand again, this time, she realized as needles of guilt pricked at her heart, a squeeze of apology for what she was about to do.

As Uncle savored his sweet—sneaking bits of raspberry filling to Merlin when he thought she wasn't looking—Flan slipped from his bedchamber and into the workshop, pulled the thick curtain fast behind her, and quietly set to work.

She first stoked the stove to a crackling blaze, for she would need the heat to help fashion the silver. From Uncle's vast shelves she gathered the tools she would use to craft the components. From her string bag she pulled the materials she'd procured at the apothecary and the jeweler and arranged them next to the stack of books she'd collected about vampires.

Obsidian leaped to the table and paced the length of it, sniffing each item: dried yew leaves, extract of holly, a bar of lead, a small steel spring, a length of velvet, a fist-sized silver nugget, and two finely cut rubies. Flan only hoped the stranger spoke the truth when he said he was willing to pay, no matter the cost. The jeweler had been none too eager to put the silver and rubies on Uncle's account.

She warmed her hands before the fire, drew in a breath, and settled onto her stool. She'd set out *A Practical Guide to Vampires* before she'd left the shop that morning, but as she opened the book to the page she'd marked, her fingers trembled and her heart beat so high in her throat, she feared it would choke her.

"Crone's nightgown," she whispered. "It's simply a talisman."

Obsidian hissed, and Flan had to grant he had a point. It was *not* simply a talisman. It was a Talisman of Undead Mastery, a very specific sort of Talisman of Undead Mastery, fashioned for the stranger, who was, in all likelihood, a vampire hunter. It required her full concentration and the most powerful magic she'd ever attempted.

It required that she break the promise she'd made to Uncle as he lay fevered and on the brink of collapse.

"But that was before I knew," she insisted. "Before anyone suspected a vampire, least of all Uncle. If he knew, he would understand. He would know I have no choice."

Obsidian swished his tail.

"No," she told him. "I can't waltz into Uncle's sickroom and tell him. He's too weak. And if he knew a vampire stalked the city, he would crawl from his sickbed to stop him, with no regard for his own health. I want to cure my uncle, Obsidian, not send him to his grave." She turned back to the *Practical Guide.* "Little wonder my fingers tremble."

Flan read the description of the talisman, made careful note of the specific instructions the stranger had given her, and, using the stove to heat the silver, began fashioning a fist-sized nugget into the shape of a skull.

She worked as quietly as she knew how, hammering softly while keeping one ear primed for sounds from the other room, sounds of Uncle's racking cough, or his fevered moan, or the scuffle of his footsteps should he become strong enough to come see what she was about.

She employed her tools with all the skill she could muster, for she knew that the size, the depth, the very curve of the skull could mean the difference between success and failure.

She had no more than finished shaping the silver when a sharp rap startled her from her creative fervor.

She sat up. Obsidian pricked an ear.

The rap sounded again.

Flan wrapped the skull in a square of soft flannel and tucked it into a long-forgotten drawer in the corner. She brushed the hair from her face and mopped the sweat from her brow, then scooped Obsidian into her arms and slipped from the workshop and down the steps.

Halfway downstairs, she heard the rapping again.

"I'm coming," she called out.

She skittered into the bookshop and through the aisles of shelves. When she reached the front door, she peered out——and saw no one.

"Odd."

She unspelled the lock and eased the door open enough to poke out her head. A fine rain had begun to fall, and icy mist peppered her face. She glanced first one direction, then the other.

And caught a flash of green silk and long red hair scuttling away through the drizzle. The figure cast a quick glance over its shoulder, revealing a cheek mottled and rough, the skin nearly reptilian.

"Madame!" Flan kept her cry to no more than a whisper, for she knew how quick the troll was to anger. She pushed her way through the door. "Madame LaGrange!"

But the good madame slipped past the butcher's, around a corner, and out of sight.

Flan shook her head. "*Very* odd." She turned to go back inside.

That's when she saw it—a thin package wrapped in thick brown paper, the same sort of paper that had been twisted around Madame LaGrange's black powder, and tied with a length of string. It lay at the bottom of the steps outside the door, nearly hidden by a skitter of windswept brown leaves, the paper splattered and darkened by the rain.

With her boot, Flan swept away the leaves and gave the package a nudge. It did not seem dangerous. Or alive. She bent low and, after another quick glance to see that no one was watching, snatched up the package. She slipped into the shop and locked the door behind her.

Flan set the package on the work counter, let Obsidian slip through her arms to give the brown paper a thorough sniff, and rustled through drawers until she unearthed a pair of scissors. She snipped the string from the package and unfolded the paper.

Inside lay a well-worn book. Flan frowned. It did not seem the sort of gift Madame LaGrange would bestow. Then again, she could think of no gift Madame LaGrange would freely bestow, save perhaps a bloodied nose or a few mangled and broken fingers.

She ran her hand over the slim volume. The cover was plain, the type of book she would have easily passed by on a bookshelf, with a simple title incised into unadorned leather: *A Brief History of the Blakelys of Blakely Manor.*

The Blakelys again. She seemed unable to escape them.

She opened the book, and found the pages also plain—and herself disappointed. She realized she'd been hoping for a likeness, perhaps, of the various Lord Blakelys—a line of Blakelys with black hair, perchance, as black and untidy as her alleyway stranger. But the pages were filled only with dense text, with only one small sketch on the title page, a line drawing of Blakely Manor, surrounded by woods, stream, and stable.

She ran a thumb over it. "The stable Lucien Kidd vowed to burn to the ground."

But Flan soon became lost in the exploits of the ancient Blakely family. She'd bought a chocolate truffle for herself at the bakery, and now she wrestled it from her string bag and settled in at the counter with her sweet and the book.

The Blakelys, both men and women, the book said, came from a long line of warriors. They were brilliant military strategists, great horsemen, fierce in battle, never surrendering, never retreating, never backing down. Legend claimed they were no mere mortals, but instead had the hearts of lions beating in their chests.

Warriors. Both the women and the men. Flan stared at the drizzle snaking down the bookshop windows. What it must have been like to be a fierce Blakely warrior, storming into battle. She imagined a powerful steed beneath her, a trusty sword at her side. Her muscles would be tensed, her face hardened, her hair streaming behind her as she charged, unflinching, toward the enemy. Would she have the courage? Did she possess the heart of a lion?

She liked to think she did. All her life, when she'd read tales of adventure pulled from Uncle's shelves, or when she and Gwen had invented their own tales of adventure beneath the bookshop stairs, she was never the damsel in distress, awaiting her strong and valiant rescuer.

She had been the strong and valiant rescuer. She was fearless. She was noble. She vanquished evil using the only weapons at her disposal—her keen wit and powerful magic.

Oh, yes. Her keen wit and powerful magic were serving her well at the moment. Evil—true evil—had struck her uncle, and there was nothing she could do to help him except to aid the handsome vampire hunter.

She glanced at the stairs and sighed. She had scarcely completed any work at all on the talisman—the talisman the stranger would be returning for the very next night. And she had promised to create two bone rings as well. She should get back to her work, but she could not resist reading just one more page.

She ran her finger down the long line of names on the Blakely family tree, a tree that abruptly ended with Xander, seventh Viscount Blakely.

Xander Blakely cut a fine figure wherever he ventured, whether tending his fine steeds in the Blakely stables or greeting kings in the world's finest palaces. With his grace and charm, most expected that when he married, his bride would be of the most noble birth.

But Xander possessed a fierce independent streak, and rarely did what was expected. He met the woman he would marry in the very textile market the Blakelys had built. Xander was first enchanted with her skill at working fine lace

Lace? Flan blinked. She had passed a laceworks as she threaded through the alleyways of the textile market on her way to Madame LaGrange's. At least, she thought it was a laceworks. The faded and broken sign began with a large *E*—or *F*—and ended *ACE*. Could it have been the same laceworks? Had she traveled the same path Xander

Blakely had traveled when he'd met his bride those many years ago?

She took a bite of her truffle and turned back to the book.

Xander was first enchanted with her skill at working fine lace, then became enchanted with Katarina herself, and soon they were wed.

Katarina. Flan ran a finger over the name. Wicker Street folk spoke of her—in scornful tones, as the woman who had brought the viscount to his doom—but if they had ever mentioned the woman's name, Flan had never heard it.

Until now. Katarina. Yes. It rolled nicely off the tongue. It was just the sort of name for a lace maker who would sweep a Viscount Blakely off his feet.

But their happiness lasted only a year. Xander Blakely, fierce wizard, staunch protector, fearless vampire hunter, met his death defending the woman he loved from the nemesis he'd cast from the city in disgrace, the nemesis who returned a year later, vowing to take Katarina for his own.

Locked in duel on the high parapets of Blakely Manor, Lord Blakely sought to save Katarina with no thought to protecting himself, and in so doing, plunged from the parapets to his death on the spiked iron fencing that encircled the courtyard below.

"Ewww." Flan set down her truffle, no longer hungry. "How gruesome."

She slid her finger back through the family tree, tracing various branches. Over the centuries, it seemed, some of the Blakelys had ventured off to seek their fortunes in distant lands.

"This Adrian, the new viscount, must be descended from one of them," she told Obsidian. "There seems no other way for him to be a Blakely."

The cat let out a low mewl.

Flan rubbed her eyes. It was late. She was exhausted. There was no sense trying to finish the talisman tonight. As she turned to make her way back across the shop, she caught a quick movement out of the corner of her eye. She turned, held her lamp high, and saw it again. It was not her imagination. She did not feel the sharp chill, nor the quick flutter of wind, as she had the day Uncle had been cursed with the bells, but at the edge of the shopfront windows she glimpsed a snap of black.

She quickly blew out her lamp, rattled the door handle once more to make sure the lock had caught, then felt her way back through the shop and up the stairs in total darkness.

That night, Flan slept in fits and starts. Her mind churned over the flapping black shadows, Uncle's curse, and her own magic. She rolled over on her pillow. If only she could cast a sleep spell on herself.

She woke as the clock tower struck midnight, but the tolling bells were not what had awoken her. As she lay in the dark, listening, the sound once again drifted into her bedchamber, the haunting strains of a violin melody.

"The music," she whispered. "The violin music that kept Therese and Gwen safe."

She closed her eyes and the music swirled around her, swaddling her like a blanket, pulling the churning thoughts from her head as she drifted, finally, into a restful sleep.

Early the next morning, Flan was startled from her bed by insistent banging on the bookshop door.

She pulled her bed jacket around her and stumbled downstairs, Obsidian in her wake. She found Therese shivering in the fog outside the shop.

Flan flung open the door, and a trembling Therese fell into her arms.

"It's Gwen," she said. "She never made it home last night. All we can find of her is a shoe, lying outside the dressmaker's shop."

"A shoe?" said Flan.

Therese nodded. "And a few drops of blood on the cobblestones."

Fourteen

Flan raced through the dank, gray dawn, from Wicker Street to Threadneedle Alley. What had she done? Gwen had come to her, asked for her help, and Flan had given her a moonstone. A pebble! And what had Flan been doing while Gwen braved the dark, fog-cloaked streets of the city alone? Eating truffles. Reading a useless book about a useless family, and eating truffles.

The dressmaker's shop was tucked away between the milliner's and the weaver's. A throng of townspeople clogged the whole of Threadneedle Alley and spilled back into Wicker Street. A low rumble of fretful voices echoed through the dark, narrow lane.

One voice rose above the others, a woman's, an anguished sob Flan recognized, crying, "My girl! My Gwennie! Please help me. Someone's taken my Gwen!"

Flan had bolted from the shop the moment she'd heard Gwen's name, not stopping to don her cloak, and now the wind plucked at her thin frock. But Flan scarcely noticed the cold. She wormed her way between ample hips and sharp elbows and found herself near the front of the crowd, directly behind Mr. Jenks, the tavern keep. Townspeople murmured and whispered around her, and Flan kept hearing one name, breathed in hushed tones:

"We haven't had such trouble on Wicker Street since, since . . . Lucien Kidd."

"That's what I been thinking. I thought we were well rid of the likes of him long ago, but it's almost like he, like that . . . Lucien Kidd, like he's back."

"Hush! Don't even whisper his name. We have enough trouble already without saying . . . *his name* out loud. That's like inviting evil."

Lucien Kidd. Flan shuddered. She had herself been trying not to think his name. Surely once he'd slain his enemy, Xander Blakely, his quarrel with this place was done.

But if he *had* returned, it would explain much. She closed her eyes. Why couldn't she have figured it out before? Before Gwen, before she'd—

Flan shook her head. She couldn't let herself think what had happened to Gwen. She wrenched her neck this way and that, trying to see over Mr. Jenks's stocky shoulders and thick head, finally squeezing past him, and spied what the crowd gawked at—a black boot, lying on the cobblestones, still laced and tied at the top. Beside it, the sobbing woman had collapsed to her knees on the hard stone walk, her hands covering her face, her body shaking. A man stood behind her, clutching her shoulder, his face twisted in agony, one arm shriveled at his side.

Gwen's parents, her mother and father. Flan clapped a

palm against her mouth. She couldn't imagine what sorrow racked them. She wanted to go to them, do some small bit to help them. There was a time when she could have done that.

She could not do it anymore. She could not even let them see her.

The throng hung back, forming a small circle around the three of them—two anguished parents and one forlorn leather boot—whether out of reverence or fear, Flan couldn't say. Probably a good bit of both, as no one wanted to risk succumbing to whatever evil had felled the boot's owner.

Flan peered down at it. It was a woman's boot, yes, in the style Gwen usually wore. But were they certain, truly certain, the boot was Gwen's? Hope fluttered in Flan's chest. She remembered Gwen's feet. They were small, with delicate ankles, so delicate that beside them, Flan's feet looked like river barges. And the laces of Gwen's boots were distinctive. Gwen was left-handed. When she tied her shoes, the bows were backward. It was entirely possible that this boot did not belong to Gwen at all.

Flan crouched low on the cobblestones to get a better look—

—and her heart sank.

The boot *was* dainty, much smaller than Flan's. It was worn, of course, for a dressmaker's apprentice could scarcely spare the money for a new pair, but it was clean and polished and well-mended, just as Gwen's boot would be. And at the top was a neat, precise, left-handed bow.

And Therese had been right. On the smooth-worn cobblestones surrounding the boot lay a circle of dried, rust-colored dots.

Blood. Droplets of blood, just as Flan had scryed in her teacup.

Flan swallowed. Without those specks of rust, it was just a boot. With them, it was something else entirely.

A bitter gust of wind swept down the lane. Flan shivered and sank back into the crowd, but it was not the wind that made her cold.

Behind her, a voice rang out. "Monsieur Anatole. We must get Monsieur Anatole." It was Therese. She elbowed her way through the crowd. "Gwen asked Monsieur to help us. He was supposed to give us bone rings today to protect us."

"Begging your pardon. But I don't see how he could help." The butcher stepped forward. He drew himself up to his full height, roughly the same height as Flan, and tugged up his belt. He turned to address the crowd. "I've been to see Monsieur Anatole twice this week already about the vile intruder in my shop. Fat lot of good it did me."

The crowd murmured in agreement.

Flan's heart beat faster. She squeezed through the crowd till she faced the butcher. "So the things I, I mean my uncle, gave you—they didn't work?"

The butcher, taken aback by her sudden appearance, rubbed a hand over his face. "Maybe we weren't as careful as we might have been. What with the new Lord Blakely fresh arrived and all, we figured any kind of creature would be scared off and we wouldn't have no more trouble."

His wife nodded. "We did try. We hung the bells. In a stout breeze, like you said."

"And the garlic here and there," said the butcher. "And sprinkled the ash."

"But the bells, well, they was a tad loud," Mrs. MacDougal said. "The folks in the next-door shops, they complained. And the mirror, well, with all the bad luck we've been having lately, I didn't want to invite seven years more of it by setting my good mirror out, just asking to be broken. So I kept it upstairs on the chest of drawers, like always. I did turn it glass side up, though."

"She did." The butcher nodded. "But the intruder came back."

"Imagine that," Flan murmured.

"It's no intruder." The butcher's wife lowered her voice to a whisper—a whisper that carried across the crowded, windswept lane. "It's a vampire, is what it is. I sussed it out—the blood, me poor old cat, and now the young Wicker Street girls. What else could it be? And old Anatole's charms and amulets are useless against something like that."

Rage boiled through Flan's veins.

"Useless? *Useless?*" Flan drew herself up to her full height, clenched her fists, and looked the butcher in the eye. "It may have been more use if you'd actually listened to me. You can't throw out the charms and then blame Uncle Anatole when it all goes amiss."

Flan glared at the butcher.

But the crowd, it seemed, was against her.

"No. MacDougal's got the right of it." Mr. Jenks shook his head. "I don't like to say it, but the old wizard's magic doesn't seem to be up to the task. Hasn't been for a long time if we're being truthful." He shot a glance at Gwen's father.

"And I'll not have it." Mr. Lindstrom's voice boomed through the crowd. "I'll not have Anatole anywhere near my daughter."

"But that's not fair," said Flan. "He—he didn't even—it's not his fault."

"Fair or not," said Mrs. MacDougal, "I haven't seen hide nor hair of Miss Nibbles, for all Anatole's location spells."

Flan raked a hand through her hair. They didn't understand. She was doing the best she could.

She closed her eyes. That was precisely the trouble—she was doing her best, and her best wasn't good enough. She had thought to protect Uncle, to save his reputation, and she'd only made things worse. They were blaming him for things he could not control, things not of his doing, things he knew nothing about.

Things Flan, in his name, had wrought.

And because of her, because all she had was a moonstone, Gwen was missing.

She faced the butcher and his wife. "If you don't have faith in Monsieur Anatole's help, whose help do you have faith in?" she said. "The gossipy women who gather round your shop?"

The butcher hiked up his belt again. He turned to the crowd. "We've got all the help we need not two streets over. Are you all forgetting who's living in the great manor house now? If Lucien Kidd is back, the new Lord Blakely should be able to protect us."

"Yes, he should." Flan planted her fists on her hips. "So why hasn't he?"

The butcher rubbed a hand down his face. "Maybe nobody's asked him."

The crowd murmured, surprised at this thought.

"The manor's been abandoned all these years, and this new viscount's just arrived from far-flung lands." Mr. Jenks scratched his head. "Maybe he don't yet know it's his job."

Mistress Cornish, the milliner, sniffed, her chins bobbing. "Then it's high time somebody told him."

A wave of excitement swept through the crowd. Tell him? The new Lord Blakely? Why, that would mean someone would need to go to the great hall. But who?

In the end they decided to choose a committee—Master MacDougal, the butcher; Mistress Dobbins, the dressmaker; Mr. Jenks, the tavern keep; and Mistress Cornish, the milliner—to visit the viscount on behalf of the town. They immediately began calling themselves the Lord Blakely Committee. The butcher puffed up his chest and appointed himself the committee head.

Therese insisted that she be included too.

"But you're just a young flip of a girl," said the butcher.

"And so was Gwen." Therese set her jaw. "Someone needs to be there to speak up for the young women of the city, since it's one of our own who's gone missing."

The butcher finally agreed, and bit by bit, the crowd melted away. Mr. Lindstrom led his sobbing wife home, the

Lord Blakely Committee set off to plan their visit, until at last Flan found herself on the street corner alone.

"Alone." She gave a firm nod. "It neither grieves me nor surprises me. I know better than to trust anyone else to look out for me. The only one I can rely on is myself."

"I'm starting to believe that too."

Flan started. She turned and found Therese huddled in the dressmaker's doorway.

Therese pulled the moonstone from her pocket. She studied it, giving it a wistful look before placing it in Flan's hand. Then she turned and followed the Lord Blakely Committee down Wicker Street.

Flan watched her go. She rubbed the moonstone between her fingers. A moonstone. Any townsperson could buy a handful at the apothecary, and even the least magical among them could expect a certain measure of protection from it. It was such a practical sort of magic, it wasn't magic at all.

Which was precisely the problem. Flan ran a hand over her face. She'd sworn to Uncle she would not do magic, and she'd been doing her best to keep her word. But trying to keep her word meant relying on practical protections such as moonstones and mirrors, casting only those spells that required the most innocuous of magic, shying away from the full power of her natural wizardry.

Dithering. That's what she'd been doing. Trying both to keep her promise and to help the Wicker Street folk who came begging for assistance.

And who, exactly, had been benefited from it?

She had not kept her promise to her uncle, no matter how much she tried to convince herself—and Obsidian— she had. And she had helped no one on Wicker Street with her half-magic attempts at protection. She had not rid the butcher of his intruder. She had not brought Miss Nibbles home. She had not cured Uncle of his curse. And she had not kept Gwen safe even after Gwen had defied her parents and swallowed her pride to ask for help.

She closed her eyes. "I'm sorry, Uncle," she whispered, "but I cannot keep my word, and you will simply have to forgive me for it. There's a reason I was given such a powerful brand of magic, and if I don't use it now, use every ounce of its strength to save Gwen, to save you, to save all of Wicker Street from this vampire, I'll be committing a sin a thousand times worse than breaking a promise that never should have been promised in the first place."

She slipped the moonstone into her boot. She had to fix this, and she could not do it by standing frozen in the street.

She turned in a slow circle, studying Threadneedle Alley. Gwen couldn't have simply vanished into the air. The vampire could have come in as a bat, but to take a full-grown girl, he would have to carry her away as a man. But where? Which way had he gone? Flan scrutinized the street, the walk, the shop—

—and noticed something, a bit of white, fluttering near the dark opening of the alleyway beside the milliner's. She crossed the street and plucked the bit of white from the bricks.

"A glove," she whispered. "Gwen's white glove."

She strode into the alleyway. Halfway down, she found a silver thimble, glinting in the darkness. A bit later, a bobbin, its white thread snaking along the cobblestones.

"She's leaving a trail," said Flan. "Like in a fairy tale. Like the tales we used to read in the shop."

But the trail soon ran cold. Flan kept her eyes open for clues—a straight pin, another bobbin, a shred of satin or silk—but found nothing. She came to the end of the alley and stepped out onto the broad boulevard. She trekked up one side of the boulevard and down the other, across the bridge over the dammed stream and past Blakely Manor, but found nothing more.

Fifteen

Flan paced the shop, the grandfather clock ticking time with her stride. She cast a glance out the front window. The last rays of sunset had sunk below the shops, and the fog had begun to roll down Wicker Street. But the doorstep outside Monsieur Anatole's Books, Wonders, and Charms remained empty.

She clutched at the velvet pouch in her pocket. She'd spent the entire day working on it, not stopping, not resting, not pausing even to eat. She'd polished the metal, set the rubies, enchanted the silver skull with a magic so powerful, the spell itself had sent her reeling across the workshop floor.

If she had done it well, done just this one thing well, she could begin to make things right again. She still had much to do. One talisman, fashioned for a stranger, was not enough to bring Gwen home. It was not enough to pull Uncle from the depths of the curse. It was not enough to restore tranquility to Wicker Street.

But it was a start. It would give her a measure of her true power. For it was one thing to sit in a bookshop and congratulate herself on the wondrous magic she'd been born with. It was something else entirely to summon that magic to vanquish evil.

She cast another glance out the window. And found nothing but aching darkness.

"This is just silly." Her voice seemed suddenly too loud echoing through the silent room. "I can't pace the shop until he arrives. I've nearly worn a trench in the floorboards as it is."

She picked up the feather duster and began absently flicking it over dust-coated shelves.

Then set it back down again, straight away. It would not do for the stranger to arrive at the shop, only to find her *dusting*, of all things.

But what *should* he find her doing? He believed her the proprietor of the shop, so perhaps she should be . . . proprieting. She could catalog the shelves. Or figure the accounts. That would make her seem smart, responsible, reliable, with a good dash of common sense.

"Oh, yes." She shook her head. "That's what he's looking for in a girl—common sense. It's little better than dusting."

No. He should find her doing something with a bit more glamour to it.

"Glamour?" Flan snorted and gathered Obsidian in her arms. "I can think of not one moment of my life in which I approached anything remotely resembling glamour."

To her utter annoyance, the cat did not disagree.

A tap sounded on the bookshop door, and Flan nearly dropped him.

"Crone's sake!" She pressed a hand to her chest. "I've become as skittish as Merlin."

The tap sounded again, and Obsidian, still clutched in her arms, let out a low growl.

When Flan reached the door and peered through the glass, she was tempted to growl as well. She found Master MacDougal, the butcher; Mistress Dobbins, the dressmaker; Mr. Jenks, the tavern keep; and Mistress Cornish, the milliner, crowded outside at the bottom of the steps.

She sighed and clicked the lock, and the Lord Blakely Committee pressed into the shop. She was about to close the door again when Therese clattered down the steps.

"Forgive me." She slipped through the door. "I begged them not to come."

The committee gathered around the work counter. They cast looks at each other, barely concealing self-satisfied smiles.

"It's like this." The butcher drew himself up to his full height. "Being's there was that little . . . disagreement in Threadneedle Alley this morning, we wanted to show Anatole there's no hard feelings and all that. We wanted him to be the first to know, give him some relief from his worries. We know he's a busy man, too busy to come down to the shop these days, so maybe you can pass it along to him." He cleared his throat. "We've been to see Lord Blakely."

"Fine fellow." Mr. Jenks nodded with authority. "Level-headed. Good man."

"And chivalrous." Mistress Dobbins clasped her hands to her chest. "I've never met a man who possessed such grace and charm."

"Huh. Maybe some of that charm will rub off on that ward of his," said the butcher.

Flan's ears pricked. "Ward?"

"Aye. The young boy what's under his protection." The butcher shook his head. "An orphan, I gather. Not much in the way of friendliness. Sat in the corner, not saying a word."

"But his lordship was polite. And handsome." The milliner's twitter echoed through the shop, shrill as a schoolgirl's. "Took quite a shine to our young Therese."

They all turned to look at Therese. Her cheeks grew pink. She covered her eyes.

"It was just like old times, when Lord Xander Blakely was alive." The butcher scratched his head. "He even looked familiar."

Mr. Jenks nodded. "Quite the family resemblance to the old viscount, I'd say."

"But he agrees we need his help," said the butcher.

The committee nodded and all began talking at once, as if a dam had burst and their worry and fear and relief could not help but flood out.

Flan stood quietly and watched them. She knitted her brow.

"He agreed we need his help," she murmured, "but did he agree to *give* his help?"

She didn't realize she'd spoken aloud until Therese nodded.

"I thought that very thing," she said quietly. "His lordship showered us with wine and fine cheeses and roasted meats and the most delicate of pastries. He listened and soothed our fears and nodded sympathetically to our concerns. It would be difficult to find fault with anything in the way he behaved, but in truth, he didn't promise to *do* anything."

Flan frowned. "I thought the committee was going to insist that he come to Threadneedle Alley to see for himself exactly where Gwen disappeared."

"Yes." Therese raised an eyebrow. "I thought so too." She chewed her lip as she gazed across the shop. "I don't like to say it, but it almost seemed that he found us . . . entertaining."

Flan nodded. But no one else on the committee seemed to harbor any doubts.

Especially a few moments later when Mrs. MacDougal banged on the bookshop door. Flan unlatched it once more, and Mrs. MacDougal fell into the shop. Obsidian hissed.

"She's home!" The butcher's wife held up her fat orange cat. "Miss Nibbles! I heard a cat yowling something awful out back in the alleyway. Soon as I opened the door, she darted between my legs and headed straight for her food bowl. She's a little thin, like she hasn't had much to eat, but so far as I can tell, she's none the worse for wear."

She scratched the fat orange cat below the chin. Obsidian let out a warning growl.

"Praise be!" Mistress Dobbins clutched her hands to her chest. "Lord Blakely's kept his promise to help us. We only just returned from our visit with him, and already things are returning to normal. Bless Lord Blakely!"

Bless Lord Blakely? Flan clenched Obsidian so tightly, he let out another growl. Did no one think that someone *else* could be responsible for bringing the cat home?

Sixteen

Flan managed to hold her tongue as she showed the Lord Blakely Committee from the bookshop. But as soon as the door had closed and the latch clicked behind them, she let loose on Obsidian.

"No hard feelings? Well, of course the butcher would have no hard feelings." She snatched up the feather duster. "*He* wasn't the one who was publicly scorned and criticized on a street corner, whose help and magic and hard work were simply dismissed by his neighbors."

She hung the duster on its hook and turned to gather the scattering of books on the work counter.

"And of course they wanted Uncle to be the first to know. But not to relieve his worries. They care nothing of his worries. They simply wanted to rub his nose in it." She heaved the stack into her arms. "As if they haven't done enough of that these past months."

She turned to the bookshelves—

—and nearly jumped from her skin. The stack of books tumbled from her arms and skittered across the floor.

The black-haired stranger stood in the aisle between two bookshelves, top hat in his hand.

Flan stared at him. "I—but, I didn't—how did you—" She tried to press her thundering heart back into her chest.

The stranger reached a hand out to steady her. "I've startled you. Forgive me. The door was unlocked. I thought you'd be expecting me."

"Oh." Flan blinked. "Yes. I was. I just . . . wasn't expecting you among the bookshelves."

She bent to gather the books that now littered the floor, but before she could retrieve even one, the stranger had swept them all into his arms. As he straightened them into a neat stack and turned to place them on the counter, Flan could not help noticing how the fine wool of his topcoat fit snugly across his broad shoulders, how his black hair curled over his upturned collar.

He studied the books for a long moment, reading the title on each spine, his brow creased in a puzzled frown. Then he looked up and smiled, his pale eyes meeting hers, and for a moment it seemed that any words she might have uttered had simply frozen in her throat.

"Well, then," she finally said. What was it with his eyes? How did they have the power to render her so completely senseless? She shook her head. "I believe you've come for this."

She delved into the pocket of her frock and pulled out a lush velvet pouch of the deepest violet, embellished with gold thread. She had worked hard on the adornment, for it needed to be fit for a gentleman.

And the talisman itself needed to be fit for a vampire hunter. She loosed the drawstrings of the pouch and found her hands trembling as she slid from it a thick bar of blue-gray metal, its surface polished to a dull sheen, its edges smooth. Inscribed on the top was an ancient protection rune, even and clear, showing Flan's sure hand in the carving of it. Flan could not breathe as she held it out to him.

The stranger gazed at the bar in wonder, then looked at her. "Lead?"

She nodded, and he took the bar. He balanced it in his hand, feeling the weight of it.

"It *is* lead," he said, "and it has the proper heft." He frowned, running his finger around the edge, then holding it up to the lamplight for a closer look. "But I believe there's been a misunderstanding. The lead was to be a case, not the talisman itself."

"Oh, no," she said quickly. "No mistake."

She took the metal bar from him, held it flat in one palm, and pressed the center of the rune. Without a sound, the top half of the bar slid upward, revealing that it was, indeed, the lid of the lead case the stranger had requested.

"Oh!" the stranger cried with a laugh.

He took the case, pushed the lid down, and ran his finger around the edge once more.

"Astounding. I can see not even the barest hint of a line where the two halves meet."

Again Flan found herself holding her breath. "So you like it?"

"Like it? Oh, yes. Very much. It is more perfect than I could've dreamed."

As he marveled at the leaden case, Obsidian leaped from his shelf and stalked across the table. He narrowed his eyes at the black-haired stranger, then touched his nose to the case in the stranger's hand. He settled onto the counter, tail swishing, and watched intently as the stranger worked the case.

The stranger pressed the rune. The lid popped up. He snapped it down again, pressed, and the lid rose once more.

He looked up at Flan, his smile wide, his gray eyes crinkled in delight. "Are you always so clever?"

She lifted a shoulder in an offhand shrug. "With spells and marvels, always. With porridge or toasted cheese or even a simple mug of spiced ale, hardly ever."

Flan was stunned to find that her mouth had actually formed words—words that made some small bit of sense. Her heart was beating so hard, she had to place a hand over it to keep it from beating right out onto the counter.

The stranger laughed again, and Flan was certain her heart stopped beating altogether.

He looked up at her. "And on the inside?"

Flan swallowed. This was the moment. It would not reveal the strength of her magic, the worth of it, but it would gauge whether her craftsmanship was solid enough to support that magic. And if the talisman did prove to be as powerful as she suspected it would be, perhaps this vampire hunter would want more magic. Perhaps he would be back. Unbidden, her heart fluttered at the thought. And perhaps he would tell others, and they would come as well. And perhaps soon she—and her uncle—would no longer need depend on the fickle whims of the butcher and his kind.

She gave what she hoped seemed a careless shrug. "Open it. See for yourself."

"Oh. No." The stranger pushed the lead into Flan's hands. "It's too perfect. I wouldn't want to damage it."

"Don't worry. It can't be damaged. Truly."

She tried to hand the leaden case back to him, but the stranger had folded his hands firmly in his lap.

Flan took a breath and pressed the rune. The lid popped up, and she slid it aside. Inside, nested in a lining of purple velvet, lay the talisman, crafted of flawless silver in the shape of a skull and burnished to such a gleam it was nearly impossible to see.

The stranger immediately turned his head away and shielded his eyes. "It is certainly well polished. How ... bright it is in the lamplight."

Flan frowned. Had she made a mistake in the crafting of it?

She lifted the talisman into her hand. The eyes were solid ruby, cut to a brilliance and melded seamlessly to the silver. They cast shafts of wine-colored light across the table, onto the heavily beamed ceiling, and over the fine black wool of the stranger's topcoat.

"Oh!" The stranger pulled back from the light. He covered his eyes for a moment, then parted his fingers to steal a look at the talisman. "Even more exquisite than I could ever have imagined."

Flan watched him, unable to tell if the talisman pleased him. She placed it back into the lead case and pressed the lid shut. She slipped the case into the pouch, pulled the drawstrings taut, and held it out to him.

"Thank you," he said, and Flan thought his words seemed sincere.

He clutched the velvet pouch tight and pulled out a pouch of his own, of soft buttery leather. He plucked out a handful of gold coins and dropped them into her palm.

"The talisman is as I said—perfect. You cannot know how much you have helped me."

Flan let out the breath she'd been holding. He *did* like it. Relief washed over her, and she found words tumbling from her lips.

"I'm glad. Truly. And in return, you cannot know how much you have—"

She stopped, horrified by what she'd been about to say.

The stranger watched her. The corners of his lips curled in a small smile. "And I cannot know how much I have . . . helped you? Could it be true? Could the self-sufficient bookshop proprietor, the young lady who neither needs nor wants help in any situation, could she truly be thanking me?"

Flan felt her cheeks burn red. "I—no—I mean, yes. Of course I thank you. I always thank customers in the shop for their patronage. How could I not? It's only good business."

The stranger stopped. His smile vanished. "Business. Of course." He nodded. "How silly of me."

Flan closed her eyes. Now she had hurt his feelings.

She took a breath. But she could not bring herself to look at him. "That's not what I meant. I do thank you. Sincerely. Of course I do."

For a hundred different things, not least of which was bringing a bright spot to these last few frantic days, giving her something to look forward to even as her life seemed to crumble around her.

But she did not say that. What she said was, "I rely on myself because I must. I have learned, through many painful lessons, that it is the only way to—"

"Protect yourself?"

Flan opened her mouth. How had he known?

The stranger took light hold of her chin in his soft-gloved hand and tipped her head up to face him. He looked into her eyes, seemed to study them.

"I've learned that too." He nodded. "I've put my trust in those I thought would protect me—those who should have protected me—only to find that they hurt me instead, more deeply than if I'd never trusted anyone at all."

Yes. Exactly. Flan looked at him. He'd said the very words that had clogged her heart for so long, the words no one else came near understanding. She stood gazing up at him, rather like a ninny, she imagined, as if she were under a spell.

And then the spell was broken.

He dropped her chin, and the smile threatened the corners of his lips once more. "I do find it odd, though, that a person with such talent for protection magic, one who is so fiercely protective of others, cannot allow anyone else to be even the slightest bit protective of her."

"Odd?" She stepped back and returned a small smile of her own. "I find nothing odd about it in the least. I can indeed protect others for I, you see, am quite reliable. It's something you will simply have to get used to."

"Get used to?"

The stranger raised an eyebrow, and in horror, Flan realized what she'd said.

"No! Of course you do not have to get used to it. I did not mean to presume—"

"No, please. Do presume. I think I would rather like getting used to you." He'd placed his hand on the stack of books on the counter, and now ran a hand over the smooth cover of the book on top. "A Practical Guide to Vampires," he read. He looked up, eyebrow poised.

Flan gave a shrug. "Just a bit of light reading. To pass the time between customers."

He looked at her. His eyes crinkled in a teasing smile. "Light reading? About the undead? I shudder to think what books you choose for your heavy reading. But you know, I've been doing a bit of research on the undead myself."

He looked so serious that Flan found herself laughing out loud. He frowned, and Flan cast a pointed look at the velvet pouch.

He followed her gaze, then began laughing as well. "Oh. Yes. I suppose a Talisman of Undead Mastery does rather give me away."

His skimmed his fingertips over the stack of books,

unwilling, it seemed, to let them go, and Flan heard herself saying, "You could continue your research here. You don't have to leave. I mean, if it's convenient for you."

"Oh, yes. It's quite convenient."

"However"—if she were going to be a ninny, she would be a ninny full bore—"I cannot allow a stranger to simply rummage through the shop. If you wish to read my books, I will need to know your name."

"Yes. Of course." The stranger nodded. "You deserve that, at the very least. My name—" He swallowed, as if the words had lodged in his throat. "My name is Pascoe Christopher."

Pascoe Christopher. Flan smiled. Pascoe Christopher.

And for a moment, she simply stood there like a post in the middle of the shop, gawking at Pascoe Christopher and thinking that his name truly did suit his coloring, bearing, and build.

She realized he was watching her, an expectant look on his face.

"Oh," she said. "You'll want my name as well. It's Flannery. Flannery Lane."

Pascoe blinked. "Flannery?" He stood very still. "Your name is Flannery?"

"Flannery Lane. Yes."

Flan narrowed her eyes. She'd been Flannery Lane all her life, named after a torn bit of packing paper, and no one had seen fit to question it. But now, within the space of a few days, two different people, two people who'd been strangers to her, had been similarly taken aback by the mere mention of her name. As if they knew something about it—something about her—that she could not possibly know.

"Is that . . . a problem?" she said.

"Oh. No." Pascoe shook his head, and his very gentlemanly manners returned. He tipped his head. "It's good to know you, Miss Flannery Lane. But alas"—he pulled his pocket watch from his coat and glanced at its face—"I fear the time has gotten away from me. Perhaps I could study your books another time?"

"Oh, yes. Any time you like." Flan gave a shrug.

"Good." Pascoe settled his top hat onto his head. "If that is the case, Miss"—he paused for a moment—"Miss Flannery Lane, then we have struck a bargain. I shall return tomorrow night. I'm looking forward to it."

Flan showed him from the shop, and once he'd left, locked the door and pressed her back to it.

He would be back tomorrow night.

And he was looking forward to it.

That night, Flan could not sleep. She lay in bed, listening to the clock tower bells ring midnight, reliving in her mind every moment of her visit from Pascoe. He had certainly been pleased with the talisman. And pleased with her too. And he'd wanted to stay, to study her books and possibly for the pleasure of her company.

Until she'd told him her name. And then suddenly he'd remembered the time and could not wait to take his leave.

She turned over, fluffing the pillow beneath her head.

What was it about her name? First Madame LaGrange, and then Pascoe. What did they know about her that her name had told them?

Seventeen

lan pushed up the edge of the blanket, crawled under her bed, and pulled out the small oak chest.

She ran her hand over the lid. The wood was smooth-polished, the corners perfectly fitted. Uncle had crafted the box for her when she was but a baby. She had never known a time when the chest had not been tucked away safe in her bedchamber.

She cast a quick spell to crack the lock and lifted the lid. She sat back on her heels. Inside was all she knew of herself.

"My life," she told Obsidian. "My whole life fits in a box."

Obsidian mewled and rubbed against her.

"Perhaps not my whole life." Flan sat back on the braided rug and pulled the cat to her lap. "You certainly don't fit into a box. Nor does Uncle. But everything I know of myself, of my family, of where I might have come from—all of it fits in this small oak chest."

She reached inside and lifted out a basket, small but sturdy, woven of willow. In the basket were all the worldly goods she'd possessed when she'd been left at Uncle's door.

She plucked up the scrap of brown paper, now crumbling with age. On the back were two words that ran to the torn edge of the paper—*Flannery Lane*. It looked to be part of something longer, part of an address, she'd always suspected.

She rubbed a fingertip over the faded script. "My name." She sighed. "And a troll in a dark alley seems to know more about it than I do."

She turned it over. She did not have to read it. She knew it by heart. "'She will do better with someone of her own kind,'" she recited to Obsidian. She shook her head. "But that's precisely the problem, isn't it? I've not the first idea what my own kind might be."

She continued with the next line.

"'Magic is a beacon. If it is allowed to shine, evil will find it.'" Flan tapped the edge of the paper against her lips. "Uncle always believed that. And I tried to believe it too. But the truth is, evil has found me anyway, and if I had been able to embrace my magic before, perhaps I could have stopped it."

The cat said nothing.

Flan set the paper aside and turned to the blanket. It was dusty now, and frayed, but it had once been a fine blanket indeed. She rubbed it against her cheek. The wool was silky, although it smelled none too fresh after these many years stowed in a chest. The mustiness tickled her nose till she let out a sneeze.

"Well, I won't be curling up with this at night, will I?"

She placed the blanket back into the basket and lifted

out a small white fabric bundle. She unfolded it—a tiny gown of soft, finely woven linen, trimmed in lace.

"My first frock," she told Obsidian. "And for a good while, my only frock, I'm sure. I was wearing it when Uncle found me." She held it up. "What do you think?"

Obsidian rubbed his head against the gown, then licked her hand.

"I like it too. You know, it has only just struck me, but this is probably the finest gown I have ever owned. I wonder—" Flan ran her fingers over the intricate lace. She stared at Obsidian. "Could this be from the textile market, do you think? Crafted in the very laceworks I passed on my way to see Madame LaGrange?"

The laceworks. She stopped, her breath caught in her throat. Could her gown have been made by Katarina, the same Katarina from the book Madame LaGrange had left, the Katarina whose lace-making had so enchanted Xander Blakely?

She turned the hem of the gown over and studied it. It was trimmed in lace, a lace so skillfully crafted that she could not see the seam, could not detect the stitching. No wonder Xander Blakely had been enchanted.

For he was a Blakely, he was used to elegant things, and he knew outstanding quality when he saw it.

Flan leaned back against the bedpost. It had never occurred to her before this moment, but her parents must have been well-off. A peasant, or even a prosperous merchant, could not afford to dress their baby in a gown such as this.

Flan sat chewing her lip, lost in thought, when something in the distance, a clattering at the far end of Wicker Street, roused her from her thoughts.

As the clatter grew louder, Flan stole nearer the small square-paned window of her bedchamber. Below, a gleaming black carriage broke through the early morning mist and thundered up Wicker Street, pulled by two perfectly matched black steeds, their massive muscles working against their yoke collars.

Flan pressed against the glass for a better look. The clattering slowed, and she drew in a breath. It was Lord Blakely's carriage. It had to be Lord Blakely's carriage. Flan was perhaps the last person on Wicker Street to catch sight of it, but finally, she had seen it, rattling past her very shop.

Except that it didn't rattle past. As Flan watched, the carriage rolled to a stop in the street in front of the bookshop. The two black steeds snorted and tossed their heads, their hooves stamping impatiently on the cobblestones, steam rising from their powerful bodies.

A messenger, dressed in the Blakely black and crimson livery, climbed down from the carriage seat. He strode to the bookshop, down the three stone steps from the street, and rapped on the bookshop door.

"Oh, my." Flan tucked Obsidian under her arm and, still holding the lace gown, scrambled downstairs to the shop door. She let Obsidian leap to the floor, then unlocked the latch and pulled it open.

Without a word, the messenger handed Flan a thick parchment letter, folded and fixed with a seal of crimson wax.

Flan frowned. "There must be some mistake." She looked up at the messenger. "This cannot be for—"

The messenger gently turned the letter over in her hand. On the front, in bold script beneath the Blakely coat of arms, was written simply: *Miss Flannery Lane.*

"—me?" Flan blinked.

The messenger dipped his head, then turned back to the carriage. He climbed aboard, and the carriage shot off in a rumble of mist and pounding hooves.

Flan stood in the doorway, letter in hand, too stunned to even think to close the door.

At last she turned it over and, hands trembling, slid her finger beneath the edge of the parchment. The wax seal popped, and something fluttered to her feet. She stooped to retrieve it.

It was a handkerchief, crafted of finely-woven linen, edged with hand-fashioned lace.

Flan frowned. "Odd. Why would—"

She stopped. She held up the gown and stood gazing at the two—at the handkerchief in one hand, and her found-ling gown in the other.

"They're the same."

They were not exactly the same. The linen was not precisely the same weave, and the gown had darkened with age. But they were constructed in similar fashion, using the same type of intricate lacework.

Flan shook her head, then unfolded the parchment. She found that it was an invitation:

Adrian Blakely,
eighth Viscount Blakely,
requests the honor of your company at a late supper
one night hence.
Arrive promptly at sundown.

Flan frowned. "Supper?" At the bottom was a more personal note.

> *Your townspeople have requested my protection from a vampire. As Lord of Blakely Manor, I am, of course, devoted to protecting the city as have the previous Lords Blakely before me. I believe you are in a unique position to assist in this endeavor. I shall take the opportunity to discuss your involvement at supper.*
>
> *Please accept my enclosed gift. I believe it will suit you. It would please me greatly if you would carry it in your pocket when you come to dine.*

Flan read and reread the letter, then read it again. She held up the gown and the handkerchief once more. The odd, impossible thought tugged at her once more, and, reluctantly, she allowed it to take shape.

She had been left at Uncle's doorstep wearing a gown that only great wealth could have obtained, and as long as she had lived in the city, she had heard of only one family who possessed that kind of wealth—the Blakelys.

What if she were—

She closed her eyes. She could hardly allow herself to think it.

—What if she were one of them? What if she were a Blakely?

She shook her head at the sheer folly of it. "What sort of madness has overtaken my mind? There is no long-lost Blakely child."

She folded the handkerchief back inside the invitation.

Then stood in the doorway, weighing the invitation in her hand. No, she was not a Blakely, but Lord Blakely had invited her to Blakely Manor. And if he were being sincere, if there *was* a way for her to keep the city safe, then a simple swish of her pen, dashing off a gracious note of reply to him, might help Uncle and Gwen better, and more quickly, than any spell or talisman she could concoct on her own.

But she would be venturing into the great hall alone, facing the eighth Viscount Blakely by herself. Flan certainly did not swoon with admiration when she heard the name Blakely, as most of Wicker Street did. A sense of foreboding began nibbling at the edges of her mind. Perhaps it was the stark chill she'd felt when she was gathering the willow bark on the manor grounds. Perhaps it was the sight she'd caught of the new viscount, pacing along the parapets, watching her.

How, exactly, was Adrian related to the other Blakelys? It was odd that he had turned up to claim the estate after all these years. Odd that he'd seemed so intent on restoring its splendor. The walkways had been trimmed, the brushwood

cleared. The freshly cut lawns stretched smooth and unbroken over the gentle hills behind the house.

She stopped. Smooth and unbroken. The house now
stood alone on a carpet of green—and it should not.

She slid the invitation in her pocket, along with the
handkerchief, and hurried back into the bookshop. She
rooted among the books on the counter until she found
the one she needed—*A Brief History of the Blakelys of
Blakely Manor*. She turned to the first page, to the drawing
of Blakely Manor. She studied the sketch.

How odd. How very odd.

Flan turned from Wicker Street into Threadneedle Alley
and darted past the dressmaker's shop, taking care not to
look at rust-colored crusts of blood on the cobblestones
where Gwen's boot had lain. She darted down the narrow
alley across from the dressmaker's until at last she popped
out onto the wide boulevard that ran past Blakely Manor.

She made her way across the boulevard, weaving
through the trickle of foot traffic till she reached the massive
iron gates. She held one iron bar in each hand and peered
through. The great manor house loomed above her, gray and
forbidding, the parapets stark against the sky, the ornate iron
fence rambling around the courtyard.

But it was not the hall itself she was interested in. She
pulled the book from inside her cloak and again turned
to the first page, to the drawing of Blakely Manor. She

held the page up and looked from the sketch to the actual grounds.

She ran her thumb over the long, low stable in the drawing. It stood just behind the house, between the manor and the woods, and was nearly a palace itself. Lucien Kidd had grown up there, and Flan had heard Mr. Jenks tell how much he'd loathed the place.

She glanced up at the grounds. She could not remember whether she'd seen a stable when the manor had been grown over with tangled weeds. The underbrush had grown so thick, she'd scarcely been able to see the manor house itself.

But the spot where the stable had stood was smooth lawn. No crumbling walls. No remnants of a stone foundation. Not even a depression in the grass where the building had stood.

"As if Lucien Kidd had finally gotten his wish," she whispered.

A breeze stirred, and a movement above caught her attention. She peered up, to the third floor of the great hall. One narrow window, of thick leaded glass, had been pushed open, and filmy white curtains billowed out into the gray morning sky. She looked closer.

A figure was standing behind the curtain. Flan was sure it was a figure, and at first she thought it must be Lord Blakely.

Then the figure pushed the filmy curtain, and Flan drew in a quick breath. For as the figure leaned nearer the open window, a long lock of thick, gleaming golden white hair floated out into the breeze, as filmy and pale as the curtains.

"Gwen." Flan clapped a hand over her mouth. "It has to be Gwen."

But as she watched, the white curtain whipped back, the window banged shut, and the figure was gone.

Eighteen

Flan ran, flat out, down the boulevard and through the alley, weaving her way through shoppers and delivery men, until she reached Wicker Street once more, rasping and gasping. She paused outside the bakery, bent double, hands on her knees, and tried to catch her breath.

Gwen. If it was Gwen, if she'd truly seen Gwen at the window of Blakely Manor, that meant—that meant—what did it mean?

Most likely it meant that she'd seen someone else, Lady Blakely perhaps, despite Mrs. Childers's insistence that there was no Lady Blakely.

Or perhaps she'd seen nothing. Perhaps it was simply a trick of light and shadows, making the filmy white curtain appear to be Gwen's white-blonde hair.

But no, it had not been a trick. She had seen Gwen, at Blakely Manor, and it could mean but one thing—Adrian Blakely, eighth Viscount Blakely, was a vampire.

Oh! She clutched her head in her hands. How could she have been so stupid? She, who had prided herself in her level-headed, clear-eyed view of the Blakelys, had been as caught up in the Blakely legend and romance as every other starry-eyed ninny on Wicker Street. The new viscount had arrived just as the town had become victim to a vampire, and because he was a Blakely, because he carried the family name, because he came from a long line of vampire *hunters*, it had not once occurred to her that the vampire and Lord Blakely could be one and the same.

And his ward. Flan froze. Lord Blakely had brought with him a boy. An orphan, the butcher had said. A small boy would not be safe in the clutches of a vampire, unless—

Flan closed her eyes. She could hardly bear think it.

—unless the boy was already a vampire. Could that be possible? She searched her mind, going back over everything she'd read about vampires these past days. Would a vampire stalk a boy, turn a child into a vampire as well. If that were the case, this Adrian, Lord Blakely was more black-hearted than she'd even thought.

She hastened down Wicker Street, only to find Monsieur Anatole's Books, Wonders, and Charms mobbed with towns-folk. They squeezed into the bookshop and spilled out onto the walk, their voices echoing along the street.

"Please, Monsieur Anatole! My family needs your help."

"All of Wicker Street needs your help, Monsieur. You must do something."

"We were wrong. Your magic is well up to the task, and we need it now. Please help us."

Flan elbowed her way into the crowd. How had anyone gotten into the shop? She had locked it up tight, she was certain. She'd left in a hurry, it was true. But she wouldn't have left the shop unlocked.

Another thought struck her, more terrifying than the first. If they'd gotten into the shop, what would stop them from tramping up the stairs to Uncle's bedchamber?

A voice rang out above the din. "Where's Lord Blakely?" It sounded to Flan like Mrs. Childers. "Where is he, I ask you. He's supposed to be protecting us!"

The crowd rumbled in agreement.

Another voice floated above the others, thin and quavering. "But he *is* protecting us." Flan recognized the voice. It was Master MacDougal. "Our Nibbles came back. Me wife found him scratching at the back door."

"That's fine for you, then," shouted Mrs. Childers. "This vampire's trading in your fleabag cat for Wicker Street girls."

The crowd erupted.

Flan pushed forward and found herself beside Mrs. Loveworthy. She stood with one hand wrapped around her ample girth, the other clapped to her mouth. Her normally ruddy face was the color of ash.

"What's going on here?" Flan shouted. "What's happening?"

Mrs. Loveworthy shook her head. "It's Therese."

"Therese?" Flan frowned.

Mrs. Loveworthy nodded. "The serving girl at the inn over in Pudding Lane."

"I know who she is. What's happened to her?"

"She's gone missing," sobbed Mrs. Loveworthy, clutching her throat. "Mrs. Childers gave her a basket and sent her out back to fetch eggs for breakfast this morning before dawn. When she didn't come back, Mrs. Childers went looking for her. Found the basket in the chicken yard, but didn't find nothing of Therese. She'd vanished, just like poor Gwen."

"Therese?" Flan closed her eyes. "All this while I've been muddling around, and Lord Blakely's struck again."

"Lord Blakely?" Mrs. Loveworthy shook her head. "No, he won't help us. Hasn't lifted a finger, even after the committee begged him. Too high and mighty for the likes of us. That's why we've come to see Monsieur Anatole."

"No, that's not what I mean. Lord Blakely is—" Flan shook her head. Mrs. Loveworthy wouldn't believe it even if she told her.

She shouldered her way through flailing arms and elbows till she reached the bookshop.

The door was clogged with townsfolk, with even more trying to wedge themselves into the shop. Flan stood on her toes at the top of the steps, craning her neck and straining to see over the shoulders and heads of her neighbors.

Through the glass, she saw more Wicker Street folk, jostling and elbowing among the bookcases, begging for spells and potions, ripping the jangling amulets from their pegs. A movement of purple caught her eye, and she drew in a sharp breath. It was a peaked wizard's hat of deepest purple, quavering above the crowd.

"Uncle," she whispered.

She pushed down the steps and wriggled through the door.

"Let me through! My uncle needs my assistance. If you want his help, you must let me through."

Folks reluctantly inched aside, and Flan pressed through. Around her she heard whispers.

"Have you gotten a look at him?"

"Blimey, he don't look himself. He don't look like any kind of great wizard, that's for sure."

"Nor sound like one. Babbling about bells and brownies and I don't know what all."

"First the blacksmith, now this. I'd thought he'd finally regained his power, what with all the amulets and spells and things he's been doing for Wicker Street these past days, and the butcher's cat come home. 'Tweren't Lord Blakely that brought her home. He wouldn't lift a finger for the likes of us. Had to be Anatole."

"Aye. But he don't look now like a fellow who's regained his power."

"Or his sense."

Flan pushed through the store and found her uncle backed up against the work counter. His wizardly robes were rumpled, his wizardly hat wilted and dull. A fine sheen of perspiration shone over his pale and sunken cheeks. A small nose twitched up from his pocket, and stroking the hedge-hog's quilled head seemed the only thing that steadied her uncle enough to keep him standing upright.

"Flan." Anatole focused his dull, watery eyes on her. "You're home."

Flan touched his arm. "I'm sorry," she whispered. "I shouldn't have left. I had no idea. Please forgive me."

Mr. Jenks pushed his way in behind her. "Look here, Anatole. We didn't roust you from your bed to watch you dither around your shop."

Flan stared at the man. "Roust him from his bed? Have you no shame? Can't you see how ill he is? He's—he's come down with a cold. He needs rest."

"Rest. Ha!" Mr. Jenks poked a finger at her. "We'll have plenty of rest if this vampire gets hold of us—an eternity of rest in our graves. You may not be worried, the two of you all safe in your shop with your books and your magic, where no evil can touch you—"

"Not touch us?" Flan gaped at him.

"—but the rest of us need protection and we need it now. We don't have time to wait around on your sniffles, Anatole."

"Sniffles?" Flan gripped the hazel wood wand in her pocket. What she wouldn't give to pull it out and show the barrister just what a sniffle was. "You need Uncle now, but where were you before? Oh, yes. You dismissed him altogether as you marched off to plea for protection from Lord Blakely. But now, when the vaunted Lord Blakely seems to have abandoned you, you have the nerve to roust my uncle from his sickbed and demand his help."

"Flan." Anatole drew in a rattling breath. He placed a hand on the counter to steady himself. "Jenks's got the right of it. Young girls. Gwen. Therese. I can't—I can't allow—" He reached a trembling hand to smooth the curls from her cheek, squinting to see her face. He'd clearly not had time to find his spectacles. "If something would happen to you—"

"Uncle. Nothing is going to happen to me. It's you I worry about."

"Look here, Anatole." Mr. Jenks pushed her aside. "You can sob with your niece later."

Oh! Flan clutched her wand. How she would like to blast the man. A Magic Missile would do the trick.

"So what do you plan to do?" Mr. Jenks blathered on in his booming voice. "That's what I'd like to know. We're running out of time."

Time! Flan wanted to spit. If only *she* had time—time to think, time to set things right, time to herself without Wicker Street folk shouting in her ear.

She stopped. Time. Yes, that's precisely what she needed.

She cast a quick glance at her uncle. He would not approve. He would know that she'd broken her vow. But there was no help for it, and he would know soon enough anyway. But she had to do something, and she had to do it quickly.

The first thing she would need was the ancient grimoire. But as she angled her way to the work counter she saw that the collection of books Pascoe had stacked up neatly were scattered around the floor, trampled under boot-clad feet of heedless Wicker Street folk.

Vexation.

She dropped to her knees and crawled into the crowd, gathering books and covers and pages torn loose, her fingers becoming bruised and bloody under those same boot-clad feet.

When she had collected every scrap she could find, she clutched the tattered shreds to her chest and scrabbled beneath the work counter, where at least she had room to breathe. She laid the pages on the floor and began sorting through them, rather like a giant jigsaw puzzle.

In the middle of the stack she spied it. The cracked leather was battered, and a large black boot print smudged the cover, but the entire book seemed to be in one piece. She cracked the ancient locks and turned the pages until she found the spell she'd been seeking. *The Transitory Enticement of Slumber*. Yes. She was overcome with an urge to kiss the crumbling paper.

Instead she ran her finger down the list of components. Lavender, caraway, holly, yes. Uncle kept a supply of those in the work counter drawers just above her head. She reached up and rummaged through the drawers until she found what she needed.

She glanced at the spell once more. Mirrors. Four oval mirrors. That one would be a bit trickier. She searched the drawers again and came up with five small mirrors, three round and two square.

She sighed. "Well, they will just have to do."

She slid two round mirrors into her boots and clutched the two square in her palms, reflective side out, and climbed to her feet.

Townsfolk jostled and clamored around her. They did not notice as Flan pulled the hazel wood wand from her pocket and began reciting the runes, tracing circles in the air for the amount of time she would need. She felt the electricity pop and crack from her fingertips, watched her neighbors yawn and rub their eyes.

At last she reached the end of the spell, the trickiest part, for she would have to cast her magic wide, to catch up all the townsfolk inside the shop and those crushed together in the street. She wriggled her feet against the mirrors and whispered a small plea that round would work as well as oval, at least this once. She held her wand above her head and swooped both arms in a wide loop, and with a sizzle and snap, the townsfolk, one by one, fell into a slumber where they stood.

Her uncle, too, had been caught up in the spell, for Flan had had no other choice. She kissed him on his now-restful cheek, then turned and picked her way through the throng and up the stairs to his workshop.

She began pulling bottles and jars from the shelves and was grateful that Uncle had left her enough willow bark and black powder. She eyed the twist of paper. Uncle had vowed never to use it again, and had only relented in desperation. Rather the way she had promised to do no magic, and had promptly broken that promise when her own situation had become desperate.

She cracked the lock on Uncle's grimoire and paged through till she found the right potion: *Protectus Maximus*. She took a breath. Uncle was right. It could be dangerous. When he had mixed it to counteract the curse, something had gone wrong, terribly wrong.

But it was also powerful. If it worked, it would protect the good people of Wicker Street for a good long time.

If it worked. That was precisely the problem. Even the most skilled and battle-scarred wizard could not always predict how black powder would react. And though Flan was fast becoming battle-scarred, she could not pretend to be skilled.

But Lord Blakely had left her with little choice.

She spooned and crushed and sifted and stirred until finally the brew began to swirl and bubble in the alembic, and a fine mist floated up through the glass pipe of the contraption. She slid the hazel wood wand from her pocket.

She stood back, squared her shoulders, and raised the wand. She took a breath and began chanting the runes as she traced the magical patterns in the air. When the words were finished, their echo dying away, she held the wand steady, trained on the bowl. The bubbles swelled, the swirls splashed, the hazel wood wand quivered, until finally, with a small *pop*, the potion came to a rest. A small puff of smoke erupted. The potion glistened and sparkled within the glass.

She dabbed the tip of her finger into the potion and waited, fearing her skin would begin to bubble and burst. Nothing happened. No sizzle. No smoke. If anything, her fingertip had taken on a rosy glow.

She tipped the alembic to her mouth and swallowed a small sip.

Again she waited.

Again nothing, save a small quiver of strength and tranquility that coiled through her body.

She nodded and let out a breath. She had done it. She had harnessed the power of the black powder.

Using a bit of kitchen magic, she quickly measured a spoonful of potion into small stoppered vials, each one fixed onto a thin silver chain. When she was finished, she gathered the vials into a basket and slipped back down the stairs.

The townspeople still slumbered. Mr. Jenks, slumped against the counter, snored loud enough to rattle the display amulets above his head. But here and there, one of the Wicker Street folk would snort or moan, and Flan knew the spell would soon be broken. One by one, she lifted the vials from the basket and deposited them around the necks of her neighbors.

She returned to her uncle, placed his great oaken wand in his one hand, and the remaining vial in his other. More of the crowd were beginning to stir. Flan reached above the shop's counter and twisted a valve on one of the hidden pipes of Uncle's heat transfer system. Steam rolled out, across the shop and into Wicker Street and beyond.

When the townsfolk blinked awake, they found themselves blanketed in a great fog. The fog cleared to reveal the great wizard before them, wand held high. They gasped in awe.

Anatole frowned first at the vial in his hand, then at Flan. "What—?" he asked, his face creased into a frown. "Flan, no."

"Uncle, yes."

She turned to face the townsfolk.

"Uncle's potion is powerful," she said. "It will offer protection." Her voice carried across a crowd that had been stunned to silence. "Sprinkle a bit around your shop and house. Dab another bit on your tongue. Keep the remaining bit tightly sealed in the vial and wear it around your neck, night and day. Go. Protect yourselves."

She held Uncle's weakened hand in hers, thumped the base of the great oaken wand against the counter, and the silence was broken. The townspeople poured from the shop and down the street toward home, all taking at once.

"Blimey! The fellow *does* have great magic."

"Ain't that the truth. I was standing there one minute, and the next I had the potion round my neck. Never saw it coming."

"I knew Monsieur would help us. I never had a single doubt."

Nineteen

ncle." Flan carried the tea tray into the parlor. "Do you
know when the Blakely stable disappeared?"

Anatole was sitting back in his chair beside the fire,
eyes closed, chest shuddering with each breath he took. His
peaked wizard's hat sat on the table beside him. His great
oaken wand lay across his knees.

Flan gave him a worried frown. "Would you be more
comfortable in bed?"

"No." He waved a hand "I've spent too long in bed
already. I had begun to fear that if I didn't manage to rise
soon, I never would. Jenks and his lot did me a favor."

"That was not their intention, I'm certain."

"No. It was not." He smiled weakly. "But the stable—it's
disappeared?"

Flan nodded. "And I just wondered when it happened."
She drizzled honey and cream into his tea. "Do you remember, was it there while Xander Blakely lived?" She handed
him his cup. "Was it still standing after Lucien Kidd fled
the city?"

"Oh, yes. It was certainly there during the time of Xander Blakely. He made great use of it." Her uncle stirred his tea, his forehead creased in thought. "As for Lucien, yes, I'm sure it must have been there still. Someone would have noticed if it were gone." He looked up. "Were you at Blakely Manor?"

"Oh. No. I was just . . . strolling past." Flan gave a little shrug, as if she went for a stroll every morning. "And, well, I saw Gwen. I'm certain. Or nearly certain."

"Gwen's returned?" Her uncle looked pleased. "When?"

"That's just the thing. She *hasn't* returned. I saw her at Blakely Manor. I saw her standing in a window, on the third floor. Well, not *her* so much as her hair."

"Her hair."

"Long, golden white, with that bit of a wave Gwen has. No one else possesses hair like that, Uncle. It had to be her. It had to be." Even to her own ears, the story sounded desperate.

"Flan." The cup rattled in her uncle's hand. "You stay away from that place. Stay away from the manor. Stay away from the viscount."

"But Uncle, he is the vampire. I'm certain of it."

"Then hear me clearly, Flan. Stay away."

She closed her eyes. "Gwen is my friend. And Therese. At least they used to be. And they asked for my help."

Anatole looked at her. "They did *what?*"

Flan let out a breath. She had not meant to upset him. She knew she needed to tell Uncle all she'd been up to—in time. But she did not want that time to have come.

She picked up the fireplace poker. "They were frightened. Something was following them." She stole a glance at her uncle. "The vampire."

"And why did they think *you* could help?"

"They didn't . . . exactly." She poked at the fire. A shower of embers crackled onto the hearth. "They came asking for you."

Anatole studied her. "Me? How odd, since I don't recall you bringing them to see me."

"I didn't. You couldn't. You were . . . sick."

"So *you* helped them."

"I was going to help them. I gave them moonstones. And told them to stop by the shop for bone rings the next day. I made them believe it was you who would fashion the rings. I didn't tell them about the curse. I didn't tell anyone."

"Anyone?" Anatole gripped the arm of his chair. "Have you been helping others?"

"A few." She stabbed at the fire again. "But I didn't let on that you were ill. I didn't tell them anything was wrong, not even the sniffles. Except just now with Mr. Jenks." She looked up. "But I had to tell him something. He thought you were out of your mind."

"As well I must be, to have allowed you to spell the amulet for the butcher. I should never have done that, never have given you the idea." Anatole sat back in his chair, his strength visibly drained. "So what else did you do while I was down with the—the sniffles?"

Flan hung the poker by the fire. She took a breath.

"What I've been doing," she said, "is magic. I know I promised I would not, but the truth is, you were so sick, and I was so scared, I would have promised anything. And the other truth"—she raised her chin—"is that I will continue to do magic. It is a part of me, a part I can't deny any more than I can deny the stubbornness of my hair. They came to me—our friends, our neighbors—begging for help. I had no choice."

"You had a choice. You always have a choice, Flan. You could have let it go. You *should* have let it go."

"That's not what you would do. When someone comes to you, you summon every ounce of your skill and magic to help them."

"You should have let it *go.*"

Flan stared it him, mouth open. "And what would you have me say to them? 'So sorry. The great wizard has fallen under a curse and is half mad with fever. You'll have to fend for yourselves this time. Godspeed.' Would that have been better?"

Her uncle pinched the bridge of his nose. "Has your way made anything better, Flan? You've left yourself open to all manner of evil, and no one in Wicker Street seems the safer for it. In truth, you may very well have made things worse. You tried to help Gwen and Therese. How did that turn out?"

Flan let out a breath. She shook her head. "Dreadfully, as you know full well. But only because I was trying to hide, trying to pretend I possessed no magic. But I'm not hiding now. If I have any chance of saving them, I have to try. And now that I've seen Gwen—"

"Stay clear of Blakely Manor, Flan. Do you hear me?" Anatole gripped the handle of his teacup so tightly Flan feared the fine porcelain would snap off in his hand. His face was white. "If you are right, if Lord Blakely is indeed the vampire—and these are big ifs, Flan—if this is true, then it is all the more reason for you to stay as far away as you can. And if it is not true, Adrian Blakely is still an odd sort, and a stranger besides. I don't trust him."

"You don't trust *me*, you mean."

"And should I?"

Flan pulled her head back as if she'd been slapped. She stared at him. Tears burned at her eyelids. She turned and marched from the parlor and down the stairs.

Flan paced before the bookshop windows. She had not meant to anger Uncle. He was sick. He was exhausted. He did not need her draining him of the last bit of strength he had left.

But that was precisely why she'd done what she had done. Could he not see that? She'd been trying to help him, to protect him. She'd been defending his reputation, his wizardry, until he was well enough to take over for himself.

Crone's nightgown! She stomped her boot against the wooden planks of the floor. He could be so vexing. Did he truly think she'd been using her magic behind his back for the pure enjoyment of it?

Fine. She *had* enjoyed it. At first. She had felt a small tingle of excitement when she'd cast those few spells, a relief, a joy, at finally—finally—being able to practice her natural-born magic, a magic Uncle himself admitted was more powerful than most any he'd seen. But that wasn't the reason she'd done it. And it hadn't been exciting for long. After a time it became a burden, a responsibility, an even bigger worry than the ones she already carried.

She pulled the broom from the corner. The townsfolk had crowded into the shop with no thought of how many leaves or pebbles they might track in with them, how many bookshelves they might overturn. She swept at the floor, nearly sweeping the polish from the very wood.

But what if Uncle was right? What if she *had* made things worse? Had her moonstone made Gwen too confident, too sure that evil could no longer befall her? Had she gone out at night thinking the vampire could no longer harm her?

Flan slid her hand into her pocket and fingered the smooth parchment nestled inside. She needed to find Gwen and Therese, and she held an invitation to do just that.

She leaned the broom against a stool and pulled the ancient grimoire from the stack of books on the work counter. She slipped the invitation between its pages, locked its small iron lock tight, spelled it for extra protection, and stashed the dusty spellbook high on a shelf in the darkest corner of the shop.

There, she was sure, no one would find it.

Flan sat at the shop counter. The floor beneath her gleamed from its fresh sweeping and mopping. The shelves had not one speck of dust. The charms and amulets and been tidied. And she was hunkered over the *Practical Guide*, making a list of protections she might use against a vampire.

The sun had dropped behind the Wicker Street shops. Shadows cloaked Monsieur Anatole's Books, Wonders, and Charms. Lamplight flickered across her list—a list dotted with ink that had dripped from Flan's pen when she was not paying heed.

And Pascoe Christopher had not yet darkened the doorstep.

In truth, she wasn't convinced he would. He'd said he would return, but he may have simply been trying to be polite.

He'd left so suddenly the night before. She'd thought it had something to do with her name, but perhaps she'd simply scared him off, forcing him to reveal his own name and staring into his eyes like a love struck ninny.

Well. She would not make that mistake again.

She glanced at the clock. "Crone's nightgown. I swear it's ticking backward."

Obsidian yawned. Flan sighed and turned back to her list.

She had no more than dipped her pen in the ink bottle when a breeze swept through the shop, scattering the papers around the counter.

"Oh, dear." A voice rang through the shop. "I've made a mess of things, haven't I?"

Flan looked up and found Pascoe Christopher standing at the door, top hat held to his chest, the wind fluttering his raven hair and whipping his topcoat around his legs. He clicked the door shut behind him, closing off the breeze, and scrambled to retrieve the account pages.

He shuffled them into a neat stack and leaned across the counter to hand them to her. He looked up, his face was only inches from hers, so near she could feel his breath on her face.

So near the scent of him drifted round her, some sort of shaving lotion, she thought, or a lovely kind of soap, something with a strong aroma, sweet and a bit spicy and clean, and she found herself standing at the counter, simply breathing it in.

"Yes. Well." She blinked. "I guess you've come about the books."

Crone's nightgown. Flan closed her eyes. Pascoe Christopher must think she hadn't a brain in her head.

She sighed and led him to the bookshelves, thinking that the sooner he began his research, the sooner she would be able to stop talking. And sniffing him.

She trekked methodically up one aisle and down the next, pulling books from the shelves.

"This one doesn't go into great detail, but is a solid introduction." She handed Pascoe *The Compleat Vampire for Jesters and Fools*. "And this one"—she blew the dust from a dense, leather-bound volume—"has an excellent index."

Pascoe took the book from her. "*A Comprehensive Investigation and Analysis of the Vampire Race*. Sounds . . . dreary."

Flan laughed. "It is. But it's a good reference. Ah." She unearthed an oversized tome with a crumbling spine. "This one's a bit livelier. Rather old, but it has pictures."

Pascoe balanced the book on his stack. "*Adventures in Vampire Hunting.* That does sound like a romp."

"And here's one you should have." Flan stood on tiptoe and reached for a book on the top shelf. She bounced up and down, her fingers skimming the book's spine, but could not reach high enough to pull it down.

"Let me help you." Pascoe leaned in behind her, so close the lapel of his jacket swept against her ear, and wriggled the book from the shelf. "Here we are."

He looked down just as Flan looked up. His breath brushed her cheek, the spicy scent of him whirled around her once more, and for a moment Flan simply stood there, held motionless once again by his pale gray eyes.

Her mind reeled. Was he about to kiss her? Was this what it was like to be kissed, this dizzy, floating feeling, her brain drifting free from her body? She had no idea. She'd only ever been kissed by Obsidian, and she was fairly certain he didn't count.

Pascoe smiled. "Was it painful?"

Flan shook her head. "What?"

"You couldn't reach the book, I offered to get it down, and you let me." He held up *Vampire Methods and Magic* as proof. "The girl who refuses to rely on anyone but herself accepted my help."

"Oh." Flan blinked. "Yes. I suppose I did." Her brain slipped back into her body. She stood back and brushed a stray copper curl from her cheek. "Well then. That should be enough to get you started."

"So was it painful?"

"I—no." She shook her head. "It was just a book."

"And?"

"And what?"

"And you trusted me."

"To reach a book?" She laughed. "Yes, I trusted you."

"Good." Pascoe nodded. "It's a start. Not everyone will let you down, you know. Some may have your best interest at heart, though you do not like what they say."

"Now you sound like my uncle."

"Your uncle." Pascoe tipped his head. "The wizard lying in his sickbed upstairs."

Flan stared at him, eyes narrowed. "How do you know about my uncle?"

He shrugged. "One hears things and draws conclusions." He gave a small smile. "Gossip on this street is hard to escape."

"Yes." Flan pressed her lips together. "Even more difficult to escape it from this end."

Pascoe studied her. "It's been that bad?"

"No." Flan snorted—not a particularly ladylike sound. "It's been worse."

"And so you trust no one but yourself."

Flan looked at him. How was it that he seemed to know so much about her when she had told him so little. She shook her head.

"Have you come here simply to vex me?" she said.

"No." He smiled. "I came to make a study of the undead."

Pascoe carried the books to the counter and hunkered down on one of the tall stools. He pored through the pages, asking Flan questions from time to time and cross-referencing each point with other books. He pulled a small leather-bound notebook from his vest pocket and scribbled notes with the stub of a pencil, licking the lead before marking down each entry.

Flan, meanwhile, returned to her *Practical Guide* and soon became so caught up in the text that she took little heed of anything else until she heard Obsidian hiss.

She looked up to find that Pascoe had finished with his stack of books and had wandered off toward the bookshelves, seeking out new volumes. He stopped, held up a finger, then turned and headed directly toward the far dark corner of the shop. He pulled the rolling ladder to him, climbed to the top, and moved his hand over the volumes shelved there, coming to a stop above the ancient grimoire, almost as if he were drawn to it, as if he could sense it there.

Flan drew in a sharp breath. Pascoe wriggled the spell-book free, ran a hand across the dusty cover, and studied the engraved leather.

"Here." Flan scrambled to the ladder. She held up her hands. "Let me help you with that."

"No need."

Pascoe smiled again—that twinkling smile that halted her very words before they could leave her tongue—then tucked the ancient spellbook beneath his arm and tripped down from the ladder. He set the grimoire on the counter and pushed at the lock.

Flan reached for it again. "I should help you with that or you'll never get it—"

The lock clicked, and the book fell open in his hands.

Lord Blakely's invitation fluttered to his feet. He scooped it up and started to hand it to her, then stopped. He stared at it for a moment, rubbing his thumb over the Blakely coat of arms.

He looked up, his pale eyes wide. "You've received correspondence from Lord Blakely?"

"Oh. No. Well, rather, I suppose." Flan shrugged and reached for the parchment. "It's merely an invitation. To a late supper. Nothing of significance."

Pascoe pulled the invitation away. "You're not thinking of going?"

Flan raised her chin. "Yes, actually." She plucked the parchment from his fingers. "I am."

The lace handkerchief slipped from the parchment, and Flan snatched it from the counter.

Pascoe frowned. "What is that?"

She shrugged. "Only a handkerchief."

"From Lord Blakely?" Pascoe's face grew dark. "He sent you"—he reached out to touch the slip of fabric in her hand—"he sent you a lace handkerchief? Flan." He looked up. "Please. You can't go."

Something about the way he said her name—and the way he looked at her with such alarm in his eyes—disarmed her for a moment.

But only for a moment. "I can," she said. "I've been invited to supper. There's no reason I shouldn't go."

"There's *every* reason you shouldn't go."

"Such as?"

"Such as—" Pascoe swallowed. "It's not fitting."

"Not fitting?"

"Not safe. A young woman like you shouldn't be venturing out alone. There are things going on here, Flan. Things you know little about."

"Is that so? Well, Mr. Pascoe Christopher." She raised her chin. "Perhaps I know more than you think. Perhaps I know that a vampire walks among us, and perhaps I know who he is. Perhaps that is my very intent in going to Blakely Manor."

She closed her eyes. She had not meant to say so much. Why did she always do this? She let her pride run away with her, and it never took her down a sensible path.

"Your intent?" Pascoe stopped. "So you think—you believe—Lord Blakely . . . ?"

She took a breath. "It seems ludicrous when I say it out loud. The Blakelys are vampire *hunters*, not vampires themselves. And yet"—she studied the invitation in her hand—"there's the holly, and the lilies, and the kitchen garden with all the herbs. Anything that could prove toxic to a vampire. He took those out. And the stream." She looked up. "He dammed the stream."

Pascoe nodded. "A vampire cannot cross running water."

"And there've been so many other things. The missing cat. The blood at the butcher's." Flan chewed her lip. "The one thing I can't sort out is the violin."

Pascoe paused. "The violin?"

She nodded. "Mrs. MacDougal is missing her violin. He swiped it right from her shop. Why would a vampire steal a violin?"

"Perhaps he—didn't. I mean, what if it were not the vampire?" Pascoe seemed perplexed. "What if it were taken by, I don't know, someone who simply wanted a violin, someone who loved music, who, perhaps, missed the playing of it?"

"Perhaps. But that would be a stunning coincidence." Flan looked up at Pascoe. "You know, I think I heard it."

"Heard . . . what?"

"The violin. The music was sweet, haunting, sort of drifting over the city. It was lovely. It felt like a lullaby."

Pascoe nodded. "A nocturne."

Flan frowned. "A what?"

"A nocturne." He gave a quick shrug. "At least, I assume that's what you heard. A romantic, lyrical sort of lullaby meant for the nighttime." A slight smile curled the corners of his lips, and he gazed out the bookshop window, seemingly lost in thought. "As if one's soul, yearning to reclaim what it had lost, has been set free to soar through the shadows and moonlight."

"Yes. Soaring through shadows and moonlight. That's exactly how it sounded." Flan nodded. "You know, Gwen thought it saved her. The music. She thought it saved her from the vampire."

"And did it?"

"Well, no. Clearly not. The first time, perhaps, but I heard it, too, the night she was taken, and it clearly didn't save her then." Flan closed her eyes. "He took her anyway, and nothing—not the music, not the moonstone, nothing—could save her." She shook her head. "Odd, isn't it? He's preying on the very city his family fought so fiercely to protect. A member of a great vampire-hunting family becomes a vampire." She looked up. "And you—"

Pascoe seemed to shrink back. "Me?"

"That's why you're here. You're trying to stop him, aren't you? You're a vampire hunter as well."

He flashed a smile. "Was it the talisman that gave me away?" He waved a hand at the books stacked on the counter. "Or my reading material?"

Flan smiled back. She pulled a pen, a sheet of paper, and a bottle of ink from the drawer.

She unstoppered the ink. "It's time I made my reply to Lord Blakely."

Pascoe nodded. "Wise decision, Flan. You can't go there, knowing what you know. It's too dangerous. You have to decline."

"Oh, I'm not declining." Flan squared the paper on the counter and dipped the pen in the ink. "I *must* go there, knowing what I know. Lord Blakely was right on one point. I may well be the only one who can help the people of Wicker Street. I owe it to them to try."

Pascoe stared at her. "And what of your uncle?" he said. "What do you owe *him*? What would he do if something happened to you?"

Flan stopped, pen hovering above the paper. What *would* Uncle do?

"Nothing will happen to me," she said.

"How do you know?"

"Because it can't. I won't let it."

"Oh!" Pascoe slapped a hand against his forehead. "Forgive me. For a moment I forgot who I was talking to— Miss Flannery Lane, who trusts no one, listens to no one, thinks no one can possibly tell her anything for her own good, who thinks she can save the world single-handedly, and now believes nothing can happen to her because she wills it to be so. Flan." He caught her wrists up in his gloved hands. "We're talking about a vampire. He's not a villain in one of your books. He's real."

"You think I don't know that?" Flan pulled her wrists free. "He has cursed my uncle, taken my dearest friend. I could have done something to stop him, but as it happens, I did listen to someone who thought he knew what was good for me, and now everyone I love is in danger. You"—she thrust a finger into his face—"you are the one lost in books, Pascoe Christopher." She waved a hand at the pile he'd stacked on the work counter. "You can't possibly know what is real."

Pascoe stepped back from her, eyes wide with hurt. He shook his head, then plucked his coat and his top hat from the counter.

"I believe I've taken up enough of your time tonight." His voice had grown quiet, controlled. "I thank you for opening your shop to me, but I must take my leave. You may not believe it, but I have known what is real for a long, painful length of time, and it seems a bit more of that reality is awaiting me now."

He bowed, ever the gentlemen, then turned and strode from the shop. The fog and the night swallowed him almost as soon as he crossed the threshold, and Flan found herself staring after him into nothing but darkness.

Twenty

Early the next morning, Flan set out along Wicker Street. Her teeth chattered as she skittered over the cobblestones, and she would have liked to think it was from the cold, or from exhaustion or hunger—for she had slept little, and had been able to eat not at all— but she knew the true reason. Her teeth chattered with fear.

Oh, yes, she had been quite brave when she'd defied Uncle and challenged Pascoe Christopher. She'd thought herself quite the powerful wizard when she'd concocted the protection potion within the snug walls of the bookshop.

Now, in the cold hard light of the Wicker Street morning, she was forced to face the truth: A vampire was a powerful being, and no matter how she tried to puff herself up, she was but a young wizard, her magic untested. Small wonder Uncle had ordered her to stay clear of him. Or that Pascoe had left the shop in anger. She'd be a fool to venture to the manor house alone.

She pushed through the door of the bakery, to buy the mille-feuille while they were still fresh. A pastry could not repair all the damage she'd rendered, but it could be a first step. She would apologize to both Pascoe and Uncle and set things right again. And no more talk of Blakelys and supper invitations.

She quickly paid for her sweet, tucked the box in her string bag, and set out once more for home. The cold of Wicker Street was a blast of surprise after the close warmth of the bakery. She pulled her hood around her face and hurried over the cobblestones toward the bookshop.

As she passed the butcher's, she caught the sound of thumping, loud and steady, coming from her end of Wicker Street. When she clattered down the steps to the bookshop, she found that the thumping came from her own shop door. It was open, and the wind had caught it, banging it against the brick wall of the bookshop.

Flan stopped. The door could not have blown open. She had latched and locked it behind her when she left. She had made sure of it. It could only be open if someone opened it. Had the townspeople been here again? Had Mr. Jenks come to drag Uncle from his bed?

She slipped into the dark shop, pulling the door firmly shut behind her.

Something was wrong. Something was most certainly wrong. For the first time in Flan's memory, the bookshop was not the warm safe place she had always known it to be. Now the shop was dark and forlorn and ... cold, so very, very cold. It was the kind of cold that sucked the very breath from her body, that chilled her to the quick.

It was the same kind of cold she had felt outside Blakely Manor.

"No," she whispered. "Oh, no." She locked the door behind her, spelling it as an extra precaution, and dumped her packages on the counter. "Uncle?" She bolted up the back stairs. "Uncle, are you here?"

His bedchamber was empty. As was the parlor, the fire gone cold.

"Uncle? Are you working?" She pushed aside the curtain to her uncle's workshop, which was as cold and dark as the other rooms. "Uncle?"

Meeeeooooooow.

A pitiful yowl led her to a cupboard behind the heat stove in the kitchen. She fiddled with the latches, which were all locked, and finally, with no patience for trying to unlock them, simply cracked them all with a Universal Unbolting Spell.

The cupboard doors banged open. Obsidian leaped out at her, claws first.

"Ow!"

Flan peeled the cat's claws from her cloak, and from her neck.

"Shhhhh." She tried to soothe the cat, who seemed bent on climbing up her shoulders and head. "What happened to you?"

She cradled Obsidian in her arms and rubbed her finger between his eyes to calm him. The cat let out a pitiful mewl in reply.

A sharp chirp caught her attention, and she found Merlin curled into a frenzied ball of fright in the kindling basket beside the quiet, cold heat transfer system. She plucked him up, rubbed his nose, and stowed him safely in her pocket.

She carried the cat and the hedgehog throughout the house, back through the parlor and the workshop, through Uncle's bedchamber, through her own. She opened closets and flung open cupboards, searched under the beds and behind the draperies.

Uncle was simply . . . gone.

Flan thumped back downstairs and through the bookshop, Obsidian tucked inside her cloak, Merlin huddled in her pocket. She pulled her cloak fast around her and hurried out of the shop, intent on asking her Wicker Street neighbors if they'd seen Monsieur Anatole.

But before she could make it to the street, a clattering of hooves stopped her dead on the stone steps outside the bookshop. Lord Blakely's magnificent steeds thundered to a steaming halt before her. His lordship's messenger climbed down from the gleaming black carriage, handed her another folded sheet of velvety parchment, bowed his head, and climbed back upon the carriage. The horses and carriage rumbled off again in a cloud of mist and pebbles.

Flan stood for a moment, staring at the parchment in her hand, at the engraved coat of arms, at her name written in elegant script. She ran her thumb beneath the crimson wax seal, and the note fell open. Three short lines of script were written inside:

> *No need to send a note of acceptance.*
> *We will all be dining together this evening.*
> *Your uncle is looking forward to it.*

Twenty-one

Your uncle is looking forward to it.

Lord Blakely's words whirled in Flan's head. He was alive. Uncle was alive. Lord Blakely had taken him, but he was alive.

He had to be. Isn't that what the note meant?

"I don't care what Pascoe says," Flan whispered to Obsidian—and to Merlin, who poked his nose from her pocket. "Now I *must* go."

But she could not go unarmed.

Flan paced the bookshop. A vampire was a powerful being. A vampire could be nearly invincible. One had only to look at Xander Blakely to know this was true. For all his vampire-hunting skill and his powerful family tradition, even Xander Blakely could not save himself from Lucien Kidd, the son of a stablemaster who felled the great vampire hunter.

Flan began pulling books from the shelves—spellbooks, history books, books of the undead, books Uncle had recently acquired for the shop, books that had been moldering on the shelves since before Flan (and possibly Anatole) was born—anything that could help her battle this vampire, this Adrian Blakely.

She was unearthing an ancient volume, its spine crumbled to dust, from a shelf beside the counter, when she spied the box from the baker's, dumped there and forgotten when she'd raced upstairs to find Uncle.

She sank back against the bookcase. She'd planned to make his breakfast and take it in to him in his bed. He would awake to find all his favorites, laid out on a tray. She would not need to tell him she was sorry. She would not need to say anything. He would know.

But—he did *not* know. He did not know how sorry she was, how she never meant to cause him pain, how she only wanted to help him break the curse so that he could be the wise, strong uncle she'd always known.

No. She wiped at her eyes. He *would* know. She would make sure of it.

She collected the baker's box and carried it with care upstairs to the larder. She carefully lifted the lid of the box. Uncle's mille-feuille was still fresh and square, its layers standing tall and creamy. It would be waiting for him when he came home.

She returned to the shop and finished gathering her books. She dragged them to the counter and dumped them with a thud—and a billow of ancient dust—beside the stack Pascoe had left the night before.

Pascoe. She wished that she could take him with her, that she could simply see him again.

But it was unlikely he'd ever come near the bookshop again. She'd seen to that. It seemed her greatest power lay not in her magic, but in her spectacular skill at driving people away.

She laid a hand on his stack of books. Even if he were but an apprentice, as she suspected, he certainly possessed greater vampire-hunting skills than Flan did, and it would be a comfort to enter the massive, dark manor house with an ally by her side.

But even if she wanted to take him, how would she ask him? She ran a hand over the smooth, sturdy cover of *The Practical Guide to Vampires*. They'd spent a good part of two nights together, yet she had not the first notion where Pascoe even lived.

Which was just as well. She couldn't put him in peril because of her. Lord Blakely would likely not allow him to pass through the gates in any event. His invitation was quite specific—Flan was to come alone.

Alone. Isn't that how she said she preferred to be? Hadn't she said she could rely on no one but herself? She certainly hoped that were true, for there was no one to help her.

Her hands were still resting on Pascoe's books, and as she looked closer, she saw that he'd marked a few pages with bits of red thread. She opened one book, then another, to the marked pages. On each, she found a similar passage.

Pascoe had been studying how to turn a vampire human. It was rare, and nearly impossible, but some of the old texts reported a few instances where a vampire could, through great struggle and endeavor, actually be redeemed. And Pascoe had marked each instance.

"Odd," she whispered. "How very odd."

Was that Pascoe's plan—to turn Lord Blakely human? Flan ran her finger across one passage, then another. They all said the same thing: A vampire could not return to human form unless he desired it. Could it be Lord Blakely harbored the desire to be human? Perhaps he had been turned against his will and wanted nothing more than to resemble his ancestors—lion-hearted, generous, and *human*. It did make some sense.

Flan spent the morning poring through her mountain of books, making notations, practicing spells. The bookshop seemed empty and forlorn, with only Flan, Obsidian, and Merlin rattling around by themselves. Even when Uncle had been sick, when he'd been unconscious with fever, she'd known he was there. She'd felt his presence. With him gone, she only felt empty and cold.

When the sun was high in the sky, she rubbed her eyes, set her books aside, and climbed up the stairs.

She hacked a chunk of the bone from a pork chop in the ice box, and spent the better part of the afternoon shaping it into a ring—much like the rings she would have fashioned for Gwen and Therese. It was perfectly fitted to her finger and spelled to protect her from a vampire's energy drain, should a vampire succeed in—Flan shuddered—sinking his fangs into her.

She slid the ring onto her finger, concealed a spritzer of garlic water in the bodice of her evening dress, tucked small mirrors into each sleeve, and sewed packets of dried holly, yew leaves, and mistletoe into the hem of her skirt. She rather felt as if she were wearing a suit of armor—a suit made of woolen cloth, stuffed full of protections.

She carefully hid her hazel wood wand in the lining of her silk evening bag, along with a few spell ingredients she might need. She tucked a stake, fashioned from ash wood, into her belt, hidden by the folds of her skirt, and, after careful thought, pulled the twist of black powder from the workshop shelf. This she slid into the top of her boot for safekeeping.

Last, she tucked the fine linen handkerchief into her breast pocket, the edge of its intricate lace nestled against the silk of her gown. Lord Blakely had insisted she bring it, and she did not want to anger him. Not at first.

The sun sank below the rooftops, shadows cloaked Wicker Street, and the bells in the clock tower begin to ring.

Flan set out for Blakely Manor.

Alone.

Twenty-two

Flan strode toward Blakely Manor, the clack of her boots against the cobblestones echoing down the broad empty boulevard. She approached the iron gates and swore she heard water burbling beneath the bridge ahead, as if the stream that ran through the Blakely estate were running again. But that couldn't be. She frowned. A vampire would never allow running water near his home.

She peered through the darkness, but even with the scant moonlight that had broken through the clouds, she could not make out the bridge nor the stream from such a distance.

Flan squared herself before the immense gates, and as she stood there, searching for a bell or knocker on the fat stone pillar, the gates groaned and swung open. Flan stared through them, toward the manor house at the top of the rise. A single light, not more than a pinprick from that distance, burned beside the great manor door, beckoning her up the long drive.

She rubbed a thumb along the bone ring, felt for the amulet beneath her gown, and drew in a breath. She could do this. She *must* do this. She could not let fear or doubt push her astray.

She closed her eyes and forced her feet to move, first one, then the other. She had no more than slipped through the iron gates when they groaned again and began to close, with a breeze that fluttered her skirt. They banged shut with a great clank that gave Flan's heart a jolt and echoed down the broad boulevard and across the city.

"Well." She sucked in a breath. "Here I am, then, locked inside Lord Blakely's estate."

She made her way up the drive, her boots crunching against the loose pebbles.

When she climbed the wide stone steps to the massive oak doors, she again looked for a door knocker. And again, the doors simply swung wide to beckon her in. Flan stepped inside, onto the gleaming marble of the entrance hall. The oaken doors whisked shut with a firm thud.

Flan stood alone in the dim hall, lit only by a few sparse candles hidden here and there in sconces along the fine paneling and lush gold-threaded brocade of the walls. She tried to take in every detail. She was in the viscount's domain, not her own. She needed to learn as much as she could about her surroundings—and quickly. She could not know which of these details might become important.

Her gaze darted over marble pillars and finely woven tapestries. Two enormous gilt frames hung on either side of the door, both draped in black silk cloth. Flan crept to the nearest and lifted the corner. She nodded. A mirror, as she'd suspected. He'd covered the mirrors, exactly the way a vampire would. They abhorred mirrors.

Flan ran her fingers over one of the small mirrors tucked in her sleeve.

She strode across the entrance hall to the long line of portraits on the far wall. They were paintings of Blakelys past, candlelight glinting off their elaborate gold frames. A name was engraved below each portrait—Mikloscz Blakely, Kristoffe Blakely, Berthilde Blakely, Raef Blakely, Elinor Blakely, Nicolas Blakely.

Flan could hardly believe the strong family resemblance among the Blakelys—the thick auburn hair, the powerful jawline, the regal nose, the intelligence that seemed to flicker in each pair of eyes. She could see in one quick glance that they were all related, were all family. And they seemed familiar somehow, Lady Elinor Blakely especially, as if Flan had seen her before somewhere.

Flan gave herself a shake. That was lunacy. She could not have seen the Blakelys before, any of them. They had all died before she was born.

She ambled toward his likeness, the final portrait, hidden in the shadows—and stopped short. Where the portrait of Xander Blakely should have hung was only an empty frame.

She ran her hand over the glistening gold edge. Where was Xander's portrait? Had he been killed before he'd had a chance to get it painted? Or had it been painted and hung in the entrance hall, only to be taken down later? But why? And by whom?

"I see you've found the spot where my portrait will go."

Flan started. The deep silky voice had come from nowhere. She turned and found herself face to face, at last, with Adrian Blakely, eighth Viscount Blakely. His thick golden hair gleamed in the low candlelight. His lean, elegant frame was cloaked in darkness, making it difficult for her to see whether or not he cast a shadow.

He smiled, a smile that to Flan seemed genuine, almost warm. "I believe it will be the last portrait hung in this hall for a very long time. I've grown fond of the old homestead." He ran a gloved hand over a marble pillar. "I do not expect to give it up soon."

Flan found herself nodding in agreement. "You must be in excellent health."

"Oh, I am. I am." He plucked an unseen bit of dust from his finely tailored dinner jacket. "I found myself a bit . . . drained, shall we say, soon after my arrival here. But I have been taking better care of myself of late, and feel quite refreshed."

Refreshed. Flan's stomach lurched, and she turned away before Lord Blakely could see her horror.

He stopped beneath the portrait of Nicolas, sixth Viscount Blakely, Xander's father, and the contrast could not have been more startling. Where Nicholas was robust, with high healthy color in his cheeks, Adrian was thin, and pale. He had the regal bearing, it was true, and the grace, as well as the keen intelligence behind the eyes. But his nose was more hooked, his chin much sharper.

He must be a distant relation, Flan thought. A very distant relation.

"But I am forgetting my manners. How rude you must think me. I am Adrian Blakely." He bowed his head. "Welcome to my home, Kat—Miss—" He closed his eyes, as if uttering her name caused him pain.

"Lane," Flan said. "Flannery Lane."

"Yes." Lord Blakely recovered himself. "Flannery Lane. Welcome, Miss Lane, to Blakely Manor."

He smiled again and gazed down at her. As Flan gazed back, she found herself caught up in his eyes, so clear and blue—and caught up in a sudden moment of clarity. In that instant, she knew Lord Blakely could not be a vampire. He could not harm anyone, not this warm, gracious nobleman who had invited her into his home. How could she have even thought it?

No. Flan gave herself a mental shake and looked away. She would not allow him to do this. The vampire charm was legendary, but she would not become a twittering bird like the milliner, forgetting her own mind and allowing herself to become mesmerized by his gaze.

She was unnerved to find that while she had been caught up in the hypnotic blue of his eyes, he had somehow taken the cloak from around her shoulders and draped it over his arm. And he was reaching for her evening bag.

She tucked the bag under her elbow.

"Very well." Lord Blakely smiled. "Shall we dine?"

He flourished an elegant arm toward a pair of inlaid doors at the end of the hall. They opened to the low golden glow of the dining room. Lord Blakely offered his arm, and with only a slight hesitation, Flan took it, hooking her hand through his elbow. The viscount led her into the dining room, a sumptuous display of dark wood and sparkling crystal, lit by a single candelabra centered on the long, heavy table.

Flan took it all in—the layout of the room, the placement of doors and windows, the potential for other light sources. Mistress Dobbins had been right. The low light did make for a cozy dinner table, throwing the rest of the room in deep shadow, creating a warm and intimate atmosphere just right for pouring out one's heartfelt fears and worries to the lord of the manor.

Lord Blakely, ever the gentleman, led Flan to her seat at the table, a table, Flan noticed, that was set with three places. Her heart leaped. Uncle *would* be here.

"Miss Lane." Lord Blakely's low silky voice slipped through the darkness of the dining room. "May I present my ward—"

He gestured toward the other end of the long table, and for the first time, Flan noticed a slender figure, nearly swallowed in shadows. He was also dressed in well-tailored black, and he stood with his back to her. On hearing the viscount's voice, the figure turned.

Flan gasped.

Lord Blakely raised an eyebrow. "Is something wrong?"

"Oh. No. I just—" Flan grasped the back of an elegantly carved dining chair to steady herself. "I did not see him standing there and he—he startled me. I'm fine. Truly."

Lord Blakely watched her for a moment. "Yes. I can see. May I present, then, my ward, Master Pascoe Christopher."

Twenty-three

Lord Blakely's ward.

Flan drew in a sharp breath. She'd believed the viscount's ward was small, a young boy. Her mind raced back to what she had heard of him. The butcher had called him a boy, yes, and in the butcher's eyes, Pascoe Christopher probably was a boy, just as, to the butcher, Flan was a girl. It was she who had made the mistaken leap from *boy* to *little boy*.

She looked into his eyes, those pale gray eyes that had so often mesmerized her, searching for a clue, some evidence that this could not be, that some mistake had been made, that he was not, in fact, Lord Blakely's ward.

But the moment their eyes met, Pascoe winced, and flicked his gaze away.

He took Flan's hand and gave a courtly bow without meeting her eye. "I am delighted."

He dropped her hand quickly, but not before he, too, flinched at the faint scent of her garlic water. And not before Flan felt the cold. His touch was not the same icy cold as the viscount's, but in that moment, Flan realized Pascoe had never touched her before, not without the buttery leather of his fine black riding gloves to cloak his hands. He had not touched her before because the cold could have given his identity away.

Flan closed her eyes. It all made much sense. Pascoe had only come to the bookshop at night, never during the day. He had asked for a Talisman of Undead Mastery, cleverly convincing Flan he was a vampire hunter, yet he would not touch the talisman once it was crafted and had insisted on the thick lead case—not to protect the talisman, but to protect himself from its power.

Small wonder he tried to talk her out of accepting the viscount's invitation. He did not want her to discover his treachery. She shook her head. He had told her nothing of his life, yet had somehow charmed her into believing she could trust him, she could depend on him, she could be his friend—and maybe something more, but she would not allow herself to think of that. She could not think of herself with a . . . vampire.

A vampire she invited into the bookshop.

Flan nearly clapped a hand over her mouth. She had invited Pascoe in. She was the reason Uncle Anatole was missing. He must have come to the shop, at the viscount's bidding, and taken her uncle.

And now he gave her a polite smile, showing no sign that he had ever laid eyes on her before that moment.

Flan returned the smile, trying not to let her inward seething show on her face. "I am delighted as well, Master Christopher."

Lord Blakely stood for a moment, eyes narrowed, glancing back and forth between the two of them. The candles flickered. A clock, hidden somewhere in the shadows, ticked off the time. His lordship ran a slender, long-nailed finger across his lips.

At last he smiled and pulled out Flan's chair with a bow and a flourish. "Shall we dine?"

Flan frowned. She glanced around the dining room. "Should we not wait for my uncle?"

Lord Blakely raised an eyebrow. "Your uncle?"

"You said—your note said Uncle was looking forward to dining with us."

"Ah, yes." Lord Blakely gave her a sympathetic smile. "And so he was."

Flan froze. She felt the blood run from her very face. Her glance flicked to Pascoe, who refused to meet her gaze.

She looked again at Lord Blakely. "Was?"

"Oh, do not worry." Lord Blakely waved an elegant hand. "Your uncle is quite safe at the moment. He's simply . . . resting."

At this, Pascoe turned away, eyes closed, jaw clenched.

"I shall take you to him later. Shall we?" Lord Blakely gestured to her chair.

It took every ounce of her strength not to slap the chair away and run from the room to find Uncle. But that would do no one any good. Lord Blakely would only follow and stop her.

Flan simply nodded, gave his lordship her most gracious smile, and took her seat. She had been stupid. She had invited evil into their lives, hers and her uncle's. Uncle had been right. But she would have to flog herself for it later. She was here for a purpose, and she needed to keep her mind clear. She needed to stay alert for a way to carry out her plan.

It would not be easy. The dining table seemed acres long, and the viscount had placed himself at its head, deep in shadow, while seating Flan and Pascoe opposite each other, halfway down, illuminated clearly by the light from the candelabra.

Flan had thought to sprinkle a bit of dried holly into the viscount's wine. Not that he would drink much of it, but to keep up appearances, he would have to take a sip or two, enough for the holly to incapacitate him for some little while, long enough for Flan to search for her uncle. All vampires were not susceptible to the effects of this plant, of course, but since Lord Blakely had cleared every trace of holly from the estate when he'd taken up residence, she felt certain that this particular vampire was.

She only hoped Pascoe shared this sensitivity to holly, for Flan would have to incapacitate him as well.

Flan sat back, biding her time, determined to be the perfect dinner guest, lull him into thinking she was here only to enjoy his hospitality—if, indeed, a vampire could be lulled.

She glanced down the dining table. The Lord Blakely Committee had been right. Adrian Blakely was a generous host. The table was filled with gleaming serving trays. He filled their goblets with wine, then lifted the lid of the largest tray to reveal an enormous roast of beef. He took out a carving knife, so sharp the blade glinted in the candlelight, and with great relish began slicing then serving the roast—which was a bit rare for Flan's taste. Servants, she noticed, were conspicuously absent.

Flan stole a glance at Pascoe. He'd stayed quiet throughout the meal thus far, keeping his eyes on his food—which he pushed around his plate, rather than actually eating it. He worked a muscle in his jaw and flicked hidden glances at Lord Blakely, but still would not meet her gaze.

"You set a lovely table, Lord Blakely." Flan smiled at him. "The candelabra is stunning, and the crystal, well, I've never seen anything so exquisite."

"Yes." Lord Blakely pushed a bit of roasted meat around his plate—he had not placed a bite in his mouth since the dinner began—and studied her. "The crystal I brought with me, but the linen was already here. It's a family heirloom."

Flan glanced at the creamy tablecloth. "It's lovely," she said.

Lord Blakely nodded. "I thought you might like it. You do know what it is, don't you?"

Flan looked closer in the candlelight. The tablecloth was not simply woven linen, as she'd first thought. She ran her hand across it, then touched the edge of the handkerchief in her pocket.

"Lace. Yes." Lord Blakely was nearly purring now. "A very special kind of lace, the only kind allowed in Blakely Manor. It is Flannery lace."

Flan froze, her hand pressed to the cloth.

He smiled. "Stunning coincidence, don't you think? Flannery lace and Miss Flannery Lane, both here at my dining table." He raised his wine goblet. "A toast," he announced. "To our guest."

As the viscount's goblet sparkled in the candlelight, Flan recovered herself enough to realize that this was her chance. Concealing her movements with her own goblet and murmuring the incantation below her breath, she cast an illusion spell in the blackness outside the dining room window behind the viscount's chair.

The illusion was very good, she had to admit. Good enough to fool Pascoe, who raced to the window to get a better view of the townspeople, carrying torches and wooden stakes as they marched down the wide boulevard toward the hall. Flan had crafted the illusion carefully, taking heed not to include any of the real townspeople—not the butcher nor the dressmaker nor anyone Lord Blakely would recognize— in the illusion. She did not want to bring the viscount's wrath down on any of her neighbors.

The illusion was good enough to engage even the viscount for at least the few moments it took for Flan to gasp in fright at the sight of her neighbors marching with torches, make a move as if toward the window, and sprinkle both Lord Blakely's wine and Pascoe's with a bit of the holly—a dried mixture of both the berries and leaves, as she could not be sure which would have the most effect. She used a precise amount, an amount she had tested that very afternoon in Uncle's workshop. She needed enough to be effective, but not so much as to turn the wine cloudy or bitter. She worked quickly, then slipped the packet into her pocket.

Lord Blakely flicked his gaze to her, clearly suspicious. But Pascoe continued to watch the illusion and, with a worried expression on his face, turned to report that the townspeople seemed to be marching past Blakely Manor toward the city center.

He frowned. "Toward the clock tower, it seems."

Flan gave a worried nod. "They've convinced themselves a vampire has taken up residence there."

At the word vampire, the viscount gave her a sharp look. Pascoe looked at her as well, but his look seemed almost . . . apologetic. No. Flan shook her head. She would not fall for it.

She sank back into her chair, hoping to seem distressed by the turn of events. She clapped a hand to her chest. "Let us hope no one is hurt tonight. I can't bear to think of my neighbors in danger." She raised her wine goblet. "Here's to safe passage home for everyone."

Lord Blakely could hardly ignore such a heartfelt appeal for the safety of the townsfolk.

"Yes." His silky voice slid through the room. "Let us drink to safe passage."

He and Pascoe raised their glasses. They each took but a sip of wine, but a sip was enough. The viscount gasped, stared in horror at his goblet, then at Flan, before collapsing onto the dining table. The goblet rolled from his hand. Wine soaked into the lace tablecloth. Rage burned in his eyes.

Pascoe reeled back in his chair. He, too, stared at Flan. But the look on his face was more betrayal and hurt than anger.

Flan turned away. She could not worry about Pascoe Christopher's feelings. If he did, in fact, feel betrayed, he was not the only one.

She quickly worked another packet from the hem of her skirt. The effects of the holly wouldn't last long. She sprinkled yew leaves over Pascoe and Lord Blakely, incapacitating them further, then grabbed her evening bag from her chair, snatched one of the candles from the candelabra, and escaped from the dining room to find her uncle.

Twenty-four

Flan searched Blakely Manor, room by room, beginning on the first floor. The light of her candle danced off the gold-threaded tapestries and crystal luminaries. She shivered, wishing she had not allowed Lord Blakely to take her coat when she arrived, for other than the dining room, the manor house was clearly not heated.

She ran her hand along the smooth-polished woodwork, making sure not to miss a hidden doorway or obscure passage. She paid close heed to her surroundings, committing her path through the manor house to memory. It would do little good to locate her uncle, or Gwen or Therese, only to discover that she could not find her way out again.

She found herself in a library, filled with more books than Monsieur Anatole's Books, Wonders, and Charms could ever hold. With all these volumes at his fingertips, what would Pascoe need or want with the books at her uncle's shop?

The answer flitted through her mind immediately. He did *not* need or want Uncle's books. He had come merely to weasel his way into their lives, to wait for an opportunity to strike, to do his master's bidding.

A search of the library turned up no sign of her uncle, but as she started to leave, something tugged at her. She turned back and took a closer look at a painting hanging beside the cold, dark fireplace, a painting dimly lit by a row of small candles.

She moved nearer. The painting was another portrait, full-length this time, of a woman standing on a windswept rise. It was clearly the rise behind Blakely Manor. Flan could make out the manor house itself in the distance. And the stable, although—she held up her candle—it seemed that that part of the portrait had been damaged, as if someone had scraped a knife against it, digging into the paint.

She stood back. The painting was not of Berthilde or Elinor, the two fierce Blakely women she had seen in the entrance hall. In fact, this woman bore no resemblance to the Blakelys at all. This woman looked like—Flan peered closer—she looked like. . . . Flan blinked. Except for the woman's golden hair, far lovelier than Flan's own stubborn copper curls, it was as if she stared into a mirror.

She lowered her candle and squinted at the gleaming gold nameplate below the portrait, almost afraid of what she would find there. She drew in a sharp breath. It couldn't be. She ran her fingers over the engraved letters—Katarina Flannery Blakely.

She stood there, she knew not for how long, staring at the nameplate.

Staring at her mother.

She'd wondered before, standing outside the book-shop, Lord Blakely's handkerchief and her own lace baby gown clutched in her hands. She'd wondered then if she could be a Blakely.

But she hadn't truly believed it. She'd thought it only a fanciful invention of her own imagination run wild.

But it was no invention. It was true. Katarina, the Katarina from the textile market—Flan touched the lace handkerchief in her pocket—the Katarina who'd married Xander Blakely, the Katarina that had set Wicker Street tongues wagging these past fifteen years, was her mother.

Thoughts, like the missing pieces of a jigsaw puzzle, tumbled into Flan's head and finally locked into place. The scrawled words on the scrap of paper Uncle had found in her basket those many years ago *were* part of an address, but the torn letters had spelled out Flannery Lace, not Flannery Lane. She had not been named for some forgotten street in a far-flung corner of the city. She'd been named for her family's laceworks.

Flannery. Her mother's family name had been Flannery.

Flan turned. A large gilt frame opposite the woman's portrait, of the same size and shape, had been turned to the wall, and at first she thought it might be another mirror, turned so as not to cause the vampire—nay, *vampires*; she could not forget about Pascoe—pain. But as she lifted the corner of the heavy frame and twisted it around, she found herself staring at another full-length portrait, a match of the first, but this time of a man.

From the auburn hair, the powerful jaw, the regal nose, she could see he was a Blakely. And from his dress and the cut of his clothing, she could tell that he had stood for the portrait not many years before. The man had a fearless stance and a slight smile on his lips, as if daring onlookers to challenge him.

She held the candle nearer. If Katarina was her mother, this man, then, must be her father—Xander Blakely.

She frowned. This painting seemed different from the other somehow. She turned toward the portrait of Katarina, and noticed details she had missed the first time, not of the painting itself, but of the way it was arranged. Velvet ribbons had been draped over the gilt frame. A row of small candles burned beneath it, candles that were kept burning in an otherwise dark and gloomy manor house.

And the painting was—Flan frowned—warm. Not the painting itself, but the space around it. When Flan stood before Katarina's portrait, a warmth blanketed her, a warmth that fended off the cold of the manor house, a warmth greater than any a small row of candles could throw forth. When she moved but a few short feet away, to stand before the portrait of Xander, the pure chill of the room seemed to suck all manner of warmth from her very bones.

How very odd. Flan moved back to the portrait of her mother. It was as if the painting had become a sort of shrine. A shrine to Katarina.

She could think of only one person—one *being*—on this earth who would build a shrine to Katarina.

"Lucien Kidd," she whispered.

"Ah." A low silky voice filled the library. "I see you've discovered my secret."

Flan turned to find Lord Blakely, slender and pale and resembling none of the Blakelys who had come before, looming in the doorway.

Flan drew in a breath. "Lucien Kidd."

The viscount smiled. Candlelight glittered against the white of his teeth, teeth that seemed sharper of a sudden, the canines so long as to be fangs.

He bowed, a deep, elegant bow. "At your service, Miss Blakely."

Twenty-five

F lan stood for a moment, frozen in place.

Lucien Kidd.

She should have known. He had reclaimed the manor just as a vampire began stalking the city. His first act was to destroy the stables, the loathsome reminder of his childhood. He did not look like a Blakely because he was *not* a Blakely. He was the traitorous fiend who had murdered . . . her father.

And now he strode across the library toward her. His golden hair and fine black evening clothes slid through the black shadows. His teeth—nay fangs—fairly glowed in the darkness. His eyes smoldered red.

Flan took a step backward, toward the portrait of Katarina. She fumbled for the mirror in her sleeve, a mirror that was caught on . . . something, a mirror that would not slide free.

"You have nowhere to go, Kat—" Lucien closed his eyes for a moment. "Forgive me. You are so like your mother, it's an easy mistake to call you by her name. It was never my intention to spring this all on you at once."

He opened his eyes again, and the red had faded. His gracious smile had returned.

"You have nowhere to go, Miss Blakely. And truly, there's no need to try. You are in no danger. You will never be in danger here. I will see to it. My only wish is to take care of you."

"Take care of me?" Flan took a step back. Her stomach retched. She stared at Lucien in horror. "The way you took care of my father?"

"Your father." His eyes flashed. "A shame you never knew him."

Flan tugged at the mirror. "And the way you've taken care of my uncle?"

Lucien tipped his head. He gave her a sad smile. "He's not really your uncle. He's simply a second-rate wizard that your mother, for reasons we'll never understand, chose to leave you with." He waved an elegant hand. "But I do realize you've become attached to him. Worry not. He's quite safe."

Safe. Flan's breath caught in her chest. "So my uncle is—"

"At this very moment enjoying a lovely view of the courtyard." A triumphant gleam sparked in the vampire's eye. "You see how I take care of you already?"

The courtyard. That seemed odd. Not right at all. Something about it nibbled at the edge of her mind.

She looked up. "Where is Gwen? And Therese? What have you done to them?"

Lucien narrowed his eyes. "Gwen?"

"The girl you took from Threadneedle Alley."

"Ah, yes." Lucien smiled. His fangs glittered in the candlelight. "Gwen."

The sight of his fangs sent a chill down her spine. She tugged again at the mirror. It would not work free.

"Ahh!" She let out a cry and, in frustration, leveled the flame of the candle at the vampire. He flinched, but did not back away. The flame was simply too small. He towered over her, his mouth wrenched into a demonic smile.

Flan twisted and pulled, and the mirror, at last, slid free. She held it up, into the face of Lucien Kidd.

This time the vampire shrank back and shielded his face with his arm.

The mirror was small. It slowed him for only a moment, but a moment was long enough for Flan to tug the spritzer of garlic water free from the bodice of her gown.

Lucien took a step toward her. Flan leveled the bottle and sprayed, hitting him full force in the face.

"AHHHHHHH!"

Lucien Kidd howled and clawed at his face.

Flan gathered her skirts and fled from the library, candle fluttering. She searched her mind, trying to gain her bearings.

The courtyard. Lucien Kidd had said Uncle was enjoying a view of the courtyard. The courtyard was near the west wing of the manor, and if Lucien Kidd was telling the truth, that is where she would find her uncle.

At the end of the hall she found a grand curving stairway leading to the second floor. The candle sputtered and threatened to blow out completely as she ran. She needed a more reliable source of light or she could very well end up trapped in darkness. She stopped to dig her wand from her silken evening bag and cast a simple light spell.

But as she reached for her bag, she realized it was gone, along with her spell ingredients, and—she clapped a hand to her mouth—her hazel wood wand. She must have lost it in her scuffle with Lucien Kidd.

She shot a gaze back down the dark hallway. No. She could not risk it. Lucien Kidd would not be felled by the garlic water forever. He would recover, and if he were strong to begin with—which he certainly seemed to be—he would recover soon.

Her candle flickered over something pale in the darkness. Flan peered closer. It was a ball of leather, wedged between the spindles of the banister. She pulled it loose and held it toward the candle.

"His glove." Her whisper came out in a rush. "It's Uncle's glove."

She whirled around the hall. Her uncle had been this way, but which direction had he gone? Along the hall? Up the staircase? If she chose wrong, she would waste precious time.

She stopped. Something niggled at her brain. Something about the way Lucien Kidd had looked, how he'd seemed to think himself so clever when he'd said Uncle was enjoying a view of the courtyard.

And something else. Something about the courtyard itself. She tried to remember the courtyard. She'd seen it, hemmed in by the ornate iron fence.

The fence. Xander Blakely had plunged to his death from the parapets of Blakely Manor, onto the courtyard fence.

No. Flan sagged against the banister. But Lucien had said he was safe. If that were true, if he weren't simply lying, then that would mean—

—Uncle was on the parapets.

Up. She needed to go up.

She tucked the deerskin glove into her belt and set off up the marble staircase, making her way, step by step, candle held high. On the landing, she found a crumpled page from her uncle's grimoire, peeking from beneath a carpet. Near the top of the stairs, she discovered a scrap of deep purple velvet, the same velvet as Uncle's robes, stuffed behind a sconce on the wall.

Her heart nearly leaped from her chest. He'd left a trail, just as Gwen had done.

Flan followed it—a small chain from her uncle's belt, more pages from the grimoire, a few hedgehog quills Merlin must have shed into Uncle's pocket, his other glove—along halls as dark, cold, and silent as a tomb. She made her way through the second floor, then up to the third, to a small door tucked behind a tapestry, a door she would have missed altogether if not for the small feather wedged in the jamb.

Flan wriggled the feather loose and held it to the light. It was a feather she recognized, the smallest of the bundle of phoenix feathers Uncle always wore on his belt.

She pressed the feather to her heart for an instant, then she pushed the tapestry aside, took a breath, and twisted the door handle. With a squeak and a groan, the handle turned, and the door swung to. Flan held the candle to the opening and peered inside.

She found herself staring into the gloomy depths of one of the manor's stone towers. A narrow staircase of rough-hewn timber wound its way up the curved walls. Flan crept inside and tested the first step. It seemed solid enough. She creaked up the stairs, testing each tread before placing her full weight on it, cupping her hand around the candle to shelter the flame from the draft that whistled through the tower. She inched upward that way, a weak circle of light in the murky tower, able to see little more than shadows ten feet above or below her.

The staircase stopped abruptly at thick plank door set into the stone wall.

She pressed her ear to it. "Uncle?"

Flan pushed on the iron door handle. Locked. She knew it would be even as she'd hoped it would not.

She heard a scuffling beyond the door, a sort of scratching, weak and distant. And her uncle's voice, quavering and weak. "Flan?"

Or at least, that's what she thought he'd said. The voice was so soft, so raspy, nearly lost in the whistling of the wind beyond the stone wall, that her ears weren't sure what they'd heard.

But her heart knew.

"Uncle. I'm here," she said. "I'll free you."

She pressed on the handle, pushed with every ounce of her weight. The door stood fast.

Out of habit, she plunged her hand into her pocket, her fingers groping for the hazel wood wand, only to cry out in anguish when she realized she had lost the wand with her evening bag. In desperation, she stood back, brandished her finger, and repeated the words of her most powerful latchkey spell. The lock stood fast.

Flan threw her head back in frustration. There had to be a way in—a hammer, a loose piece of board, some means to cast a stronger spell. She whirled around, searching in the candlelight for something she could use.

What she saw instead was another weak circle of flickering light at the bottom of the tower, outlining a figure in black.

Lucien!

But as he lifted his face to her, Flan saw that it was not Lucien Kidd. It was Pascoe, standing at the base of the stairs, blocking her escape.

"Back!" Flan held out the mirror. "Come no closer. I will not let you harm my uncle."

Pascoe flinched, though her mirror was not near enough to possibly inflict torment upon him.

"I'm not here to harm you." His voice was a rasp of pain. "I'm here to help."

He held up his hand. In his palm, a thick golden key lay glinting in the candlelight.

Twenty-six

Pascoe held the key to the light. "You'll need this."

His voice floated up to Flan, weak and trembling. He clasped the key in his hand and leaned heavily on the stair rail, dragging first one foot, then the other, onto the wooden step. He gripped the rail, to catch his breath, it seemed. The rough wood shook under his weight.

Flan's heart tightened. Her heart couldn't stand to see Pascoe in such agony. Her heart told her that she had caused it, that she had all but poisoned him with the holly and then the yew. Her heart wanted to go to him, to help him.

Of course it did. That was exactly what Pascoe wanted her to feel. It was one of a vampire's most reliable ploys—to play on his victim's sympathy.

Well, he would not play on hers, not again. She lifted her chin.

"Stay where you are." Flan brandished the mirror. "Take not another step. You can no longer trick me that easily."

He lifted his eyes to her. His face stood out, pale,

drained of all color, against the gloom of the tower. "I'm not trying to trick you, Flan. I wouldn't."

Flan's heart cinched. She wanted to believe him. But she had to stay strong.

"Oh, no. You wouldn't trick me," she said. "I would almost believe you—except that you've been tricking me since we met. Since *before* we met, I'm certain. That was your plan all along, wasn't it? Yours and Lucien's. Get to the great wizard by tricking his witless niece."

Pascoe closed his eyes, his face twisted in pain. When he opened them again, his small circle of candlelight reflected the agony in his eyes, but it did not reflect the smoldering red Flan had seen in Lucien Kidd's eyes.

"No," he rasped. "You have it backward. The plan was to get to the niece by bringing down the great wizard. And it was not *my* plan. It was all Lucien."

"But you helped him."

"No. I did nothing to help him. My intention was to help you. I thought that if I were close, and if I were armed, I could protect you. You must believe me."

Flan clenched the mirror in her hand. "The last thing I will ever do again is believe you."

"You're right." Pascoe had slowly been inching his way, step by painful step, until now he was halfway up the tower. "I did not tell you the full truth when we met. But if I had, if I had confessed that I was freshly arrived in the city with the very vampire who had killed the town folk's beloved protector, would you have created for me the talisman? Would you have even allowed me into the shop?"

"You know I would not," said Flan. "No one would invite a vampire into her shop—or her home—knowingly. Because that's what you are, Pascoe Christopher. You are not the vampire hunter you tricked me into believing you were. You are a vampire."

Pascoe peered at her through the darkness, his gaze steady. "Perhaps I'm both."

He held the key up and, with a great heave that seemed to rack his entire body, flung it up the steps to her.

Flan caught it and for a moment, considered dropping it again. What did he mean by that—perhaps I'm both? He was clearly trying to muddle her mind. Again. The key weighed heavily in her palm. What if the key were but another of his tricks? What if it were actually an object of cursement, spelled to fell her?

But what if it were not? What if it were, in fact, the key that would lead her to her uncle?

Flan turned to the rough plank door, and, keeping one eye on Pascoe, slid the key into the lock. With a jiggle, a tug, and a screech, the key turned and the latch clicked.

Flan wrenched the door open, and was nearly thrown back down the steps by the force of the wind sweeping into the tower, instantly blowing out her candle. The handle ripped loose from her hand. The door slammed into the stone wall with a *bang* that echoed through the tower. Flan found herself staring out into the black of the moonless night.

She pushed through the door. Wind whipped at her hair and gown, and a chill crept into her very bones. She was on the parapets of Blakely Manor. The very place where

Xander Blakely—her father—had died, had been pushed to his death, had been murdered. The place she'd first seen the vampire, Lucien Kidd, his dark figure outlined against the gray sky.

And, as her eyes adjusted to the dark, she saw it was the place where her uncle was now bound to one of the gray stone gargoyles overlooking the courtyard below. The wind lashed his white hair around his equally white face and fluttered his heavy robes as if they were the thinnest of paper. His eyeglasses hung crooked across his nose.

"Uncle!" She ran to him.

Wind whistled over the rooftop. The plank door banged in the sharp gusts. Flan leaned over the stone wall and tugged at the heavy ropes that trussed her uncle to the gargoyle.

"No. Flan."

Anatole's voice was weak, but he managed to motion with his head, and Flan saw that Lucien Kidd had been clever indeed. He had bound Anatole so that if he were untied, he would plunge to the sharp iron spikes atop the courtyard wall three stories below.

Just as her father had fifteen years before.

"Flan." Her uncle's voice rattled in his chest. "Leave. Please. You don't know what he has planned."

"I care not what he has planned. I could never leave you."

Once again, Flan whirled around in the dark, looking for something—anything—to free her uncle.

Once again, she came face to face with Pascoe. He stepped through the doorway. He was still pale, but he stood upright, the effects of the holly slowly wearing off.

"Please." He held up his hands. "Let me help you."

Flan stopped. The last time he'd said that, he was talking about a book. And he'd said something else: "Good. It's a start." But the start of what?

He strode toward her. She held up the mirror, but he merely shielded his face with his hand and continued toward her. Flan dug in her bodice for the garlic water, bracing herself, ready to fight him off.

But he did not touch her. He only leaned over the stone wall to wrap his topcoat around her. Flan shuddered. He was a vampire. He could so easily have sunk his fangs into her neck as she crouched there.

And suddenly a puzzle piece clicked into place.

"It was you," she said.

She felt Pascoe tense.

"You broke into the butcher's shop," she said. "You . . . cleaned up the blood."

"I had no choice." His voice was soft.

Flan nodded. "You needed blood to survive," she said, more to herself than to Pascoe. "You took blood from the butcher's so that you would not have to take it"—she shuddered once more—"somewhere else." She looked up. "And the fiddle. If you were the butcher's intruder, you must have taken his wife's fiddle."

Pascoe said nothing. He reached for Anatole, tried to pull him closer to the railing, but he could barely reach the wizard, much less hold his weight.

"Let me try," Flan said. "If I can lift him, you can untie the ropes."

Flan flourished her finger, tracing the runes as she murmured her most powerful levitation spell. But even with Pascoe tugging at her uncle's arms in an attempt to help, without her wand and without the barest of spell components, Flan could not summon enough magic to lift more than the hairs of his beard.

"Useless." Anatole's voice drifted up through the wind, more frail than before. "Been trying. Even with the cursed bells ringing in my head. Flan. Go. Free yourself."

"No." Flan shook her head. "I told you. I will not leave you."

Pascoe gripped Anatole's arm. "We will get you loose, sir. There has to be a way."

"You're wrong." A deep, silky voice thundered out into the night sky. "There is no way."

Flan turned. Lucien Kidd, his face contorted in rage, strode through the doorway and onto the rooftop.

Twenty-seven

Lucien's teeth gleamed white against the shadows, his mouth twisted into an animal snarl, but he dipped his shoulders in a courtly bow. "I see you've spared me the trouble of luring you onto my rooftop, Miss Blakely."

Flan took a step back and felt Pascoe behind her. She stiffened. He said he was there to help, and he certainly acted as if that were true.

But perhaps that was all part of an elaborate trick. No matter that she wanted to believe that Pascoe stood behind her to help protect and defend her, it did not escape Flan's notice that she—and her uncle—were now trapped on the rooftops of Blakely Manor, in the sheer black of the moonless night, between two vampires.

The wind lashed her hair around her face. The chill of the night had sunk so deep that her body had gone numb. She leaned against the parapet, felt for her uncle's hand, cold and still beneath the ropes that bound him to the stone gargoyle, and gave him what she hoped was an encouraging squeeze.

"Hold fast, Uncle," she murmured. "I will not fail you."

She felt Pascoe move closer. "Take great care, Flan." His whispered breath tickled her ear. "Do not look Lucien in the eye. Do not believe anything he says."

"Yes." Lucien Kidd's milky-smooth voice cut through the roar of the wind. "Listen to him, Miss Blakely. It's good advice when dealing with a vampire." His red eyes flashed on Pascoe. "Any vampire. Especially one who has proven himself so disloyal, betraying his protector at every turn."

He took a step toward her, and Flan gripped Uncle Anatole's hand tighter. She could not panic. She needed a clear head.

She tried to remember everything she'd read. Vampires, she knew, were notoriously strong—and quick. The older the vampire, the more nimble it became, and Lucien Kidd was no longer young.

She could not hope to battle him using strength or speed or agility. She would simply have to outthink him. She mentally raced over the weapons she still held: the garlic water, the mistletoe, the ash wood stake tucked into her belt, the twist of black powder wedged into her boot. Her candle had been extinguished, her wand and spell ingredients lost, but she still possessed the two small mirrors.

Now she wriggled them from her sleeves. She slid them into the palms of her hands and held one of them up, facing Lucien. It had slowed him down before, in the library, and she hoped it might slow him again, some small bit.

Some *very* small bit.

He flinched. But only for an instant, and then he held his chin high and laughed, a low wolflike growl.

"A tiny mirror?" His mouth twisted. "No larger than your own delicate palm?"

He swiped at it with one long, clawlike hand. The mirror slipped from her hand, glinted as it fell through the darkness, and shattered against the stone at Flan's feet.

He kicked at the shards with one sharp, slender boot. "*This* is how you intend to save your precious Monsieur Anatole? It's no more than a child's plaything. Come, Katarina. I expected much better from the great vampire hunter's daughter."

He roared, a great wolfish roar, and swooped toward her—and toward her uncle.

She let out a shrill shriek to gain his attention and raced away from him, away from Uncle Anatole, across the roof of the great manor house.

"Flan!" Pascoe's voice was nearly lost in the rush of the wind. "You cannot outrun him."

Flan shrieked again, as if she were no more than a mindless twit who was running in fear because she knew not what else to do. Lucien was used to such terrified behavior, she was certain. As she skittered across the loose pebbles of the rooftop, she held the remaining mirror in the palm of her hand, flicking it back and forth, reflecting what little light there was so that the vampire, even with his exceptional vision, would not lose her in the darkness.

Behind her, above her, she heard the same terrible flapping Gwen said she'd heard on Wicker Street. And the chill, a chill deeper than the already frigid night air, a chill that threatened to suck the life from her very body.

Flan darted toward a cluster of crumbling brick chimneys that towered above her in the darkness, chimneys at the sheer edge of the parapet.

"Your mother ran from me too." The vampire's voice rang through the darkness, its silky smoothness now edged with something else, something even more terrifying, something Flan could not quite place. "You will succeed no better than she did those many years ago, my little Katarina."

He loomed over her suddenly, his great black shadow blocking out any hope of light. Flan took a breath, willed her heart not to beat a hole straight through her chest, and held the spritz bottle as steady as her trembling hand would allow. When Lucien was near enough that his hot sulfur breath all but seared her neck, she pressed the spritz bottle.

"AHHHHHHH!" The great black shadow fell back, and along with it, a bit of the chill. In the darkness, Flan could see the vampire clawing at his face.

She fled to the edge of the rooftop and crouched behind one of the chimneys. The wind whipped at her skirts, whipped the fabric to the edge of the parapet, but she dared not look down—down at the iron spikes that lined the courtyard wall three stories below. She tugged the twist of black powder free from her boot, her fingers weak and clumsy with fear.

"Flan."

A whispered voice in her ear caused her to drop the paper among the pebbles. She squeezed herself against the rough brick of the chimney and pressed her hands against her heart, trying to still its deafening beat.

"You can't fight him."

The voice was Pascoe's. He crouched behind her, and Flan nearly retched with relief.

"You can't win," he whispered. "The only way is to flee. I can get you out."

He placed a hand on her arm, and in that moment, all she wanted was to say yes, please make it all go away.

But she couldn't. She would not leave her uncle.

She scrabbled among the pebbles with both hands, the sharp edges scraping at her fingers and palms, groping carefully so as not to send the twist of paper skittering over the edge of the roof.

Beyond her small hiding place behind the chimney, Lucien Kidd's scream became a roar. "You cannot hide. I will find you, Katarina."

Katarina. Again. Why did he keep calling her Katarina? It was if he thought she were her mother, as if he were living the past over again. Lucien Kidd was not simply evil. He was deranged as well.

Perhaps if she could pierce his madness, reach some small bit of sanity in his twisted, vampire mind, it would stop him, at least long enough for him to puzzle out the reality of it. Not likely, but she had to try.

"I'm not Katarina," she shouted. She scratched for the paper twist among the pebbles. "I'm Flan. Flannery Lane."

The roar became an animal howl.

Flan heard the crunch of his footstep, stealthy and firm, among the chimneys. He was searching for her. She shuddered, and her fingers brushed the edge of the paper twist. She snatched it up and held it to her chest. She felt Pascoe's steadying hand on her arm.

"He's lost his sense," she whispered. "His thoughts are muddled. He has me confused with Katarina."

"No." Pascoe pressed his back to the bricks and peered around the chimney. He seemed to be groping at something around his neck. "He has every bit of his sense, and he is neither muddled nor confused. He is simply more evil than you can imagine."

He stepped out from behind the chimney.

"Lucien Kidd." Pascoe's voice rang over the rooftop. "I have something for you."

He held up his hand, and Flan saw that he held the lead case she had fashioned for him. He pressed the lid, and it slid up, revealing the silver and ruby talisman inside.

"Pascoe, no," she whispered. "It will stop him, but it will hurt you as well."

In the dark, she saw Pascoe close his eyes. A blast of brightness filled the night, so bright Flan could see nothing but silvery white. As she fell back against the chimney, a scream filled her ears, and something landed beside her with a great thud.

"Pascoe?" she whispered. Then louder: "Pascoe?"

Flan blinked. The blast of light had lasted but an instant, and yet it had left her more blinded than had the blackness of the night. She tucked the twist of paper into her sleeve, leaned forward, and felt for Pascoe. He lay lifeless at her feet. She wrapped her arms around his shoulders and pulled him to her.

"Uhnnnn." He groaned.

Her heart thumped in relief.

Pascoe tried to pull himself up, but only rolled nearer the edge of the rooftop and the iron spikes below. Flan gripped his coat in both hands, dug her boots into the gravel, and hauled Pascoe up to a sitting position against the chimney. His hand was still wrapped around the Talisman of Undead Mastery. She peeled it from his fingers and pushed the lid closed.

"Flan—"

"Shhhh." She pressed a finger to his cold, parched lips and sat listening for any sound, any movement.

She heard only the whistle of the wind across the parapet.

Had he done it? Had Pascoe vanquished the vampire? She scarcely allowed herself to believe it was true. She scarcely allowed herself to take a breath.

She blinked again to clear the spots from her eyes, and peered around the corner of the chimney.

And saw a movement, just a flutter at first, black on black. Then Lucien Kidd rose from the rooftop, tall and powerful against the dark of the sky. His eyes blazed red with rage.

Flan clapped her hand over her mouth to smother a scream. She leaned back against the chimney and held the paper close, trying not to fumble it as she untwisted the end.

"Katarina. Come out, come out, wherever you are." Lucien's voice was suddenly close. Too close. She had not heard his footstep.

"I am not Katarina," she said. Her jaw clenched. "I am Flan."

"Oh, but you *are* Katarina, just as your mother was. Named by your father to honor your mother. Even as a baby you were the image of her. Isn't that convenient?"

Flan leaned out from her hiding place behind the chimney and, holding the paper low to the ground, poured a mound of black powder onto the pebbles near to the edge of the rooftop. The sharp scent of the powder pricked her nose.

"Stay," she whispered to it. "Do not blow away in the fierce wind."

"Katarina. How does it feel to be the last of the mighty Blakelys? Oh!" A soft footstep crunched against the pebble. "But I misspeak. The Blakelys weren't so mighty after all, were they? They've been brought down, the whole clan of them, by a lowborn stablemaster's boy. I slew the golden son, tried to make off with his bride—although that didn't work out quite as I'd planned. She just would not cooperate, and I can't think why. It was such a good plan. But no matter. I now have the chance to do it all over again, with the last remaining piece of the Blakely dynasty—Xander's daughter, young Katarina Maria Alexandra Blakely."

Lucien's mad animal howl filled the air, and Flan found herself trembling against the rough brick of the chimney. Katarina Maria Alexandra Blakely?

The crunch of a footstep fell before her. Flan saw the gleam of a slender black boot near to where she'd poured the black powder. She looked up, at Lucien Kidd, his eyes red-hot embers, his face contorted in fury.

"Your mother was beautiful, just as you are beautiful."

He ran an icy finger along her cheek, and Flan froze.

"But your mother was a fool." He dropped his hand from her face and smiled his horrible smile. His fangs, fully extended, glinted white in the darkness. "Even after I'd killed your father, she still believed there could be something more powerful in this world than I—your so-called uncle, if you can believe it. She thought the great Monsieur Anatole could keep you from me. But he could not even keep you from practicing a few rather unsuccessful sleep spells. How is your foot, by the way? Still tingling?"

Flan froze. The sleep spells. She had secretly been practicing spells. Uncle had warned her. The note in her basket had said magic was a beacon, that it would draw evil. But she had defied the warning, defied Uncle—

"Ah, yes. I see you're putting it all together." Lucien let out a howl. "You drew me to you with your magic. And now we see how great your Anatole truly is, felled by nothing more than a bit of wire and glass."

He raised his arms, and the great chill shadow fell over her again. She focused on the spot where she'd seen the gleam of Lucien's boot, focused and repeated the incantation beneath her breath, holding her finger steady, traced the runes, picturing the hazel wood wand in her mind's eye.

"You, Katarina, are the final piece. Once I have you, once you have taken your mother's place beside me, once you have tasted the sweetness of the everlasting immortality of the undead, I will have taken everything Xander Blakely ever held dear."

Flan held her finger firm and summoned every bit of her magic to it.

"It's all working out so nicely." Lucien's voice rolled through the darkness. "How fitting that it should end here, with your beloved uncle trussed up on the very spot where your mother's beloved Xander plunged to his death."

His sulfur breath enveloped her as the very air seemed to be sucked from her lungs. But Flan saw a spark. A tiny flick, she was certain. She held her finger steady, sure, focused.

The chill grew deeper, the shadow blacker, the great flapping nearly deafened her, and still Flan focused.

The spark flickered again. She heard Pascoe draw a sharp breath, and Flan knew he had seen it too.

Lucien was directly over her, blocking even the smallest bit of light. Flan could hardly breathe, hardly hear her own thoughts. Yet she held steady, concentrated. Cold beads of sweat seeped onto her tightened forehead, but she did not lose her focus.

As Lucien swooped down, the black powder exploded in a mighty boom. The blast knocked Flan against the chimney, knocked the very breath from her body. The rooftop quaked. Smoke and grit filled her eyes, her nose, her mouth. Bricks and pebbles rained down around her.

And through it all, she caught the snap of black, as Lucien Kidd, thrown back by the blast, tumbled backward over the edge of the stone parapet.

Flan coughed and dug at her eyes and scrambled to the edge of the roof, Pascoe by her side. They peered down at Lucien's body, impaled on the iron spikes surrounding the courtyard, three stories below.

Twenty-eight

Pascoe climbed to his feet and held out a hand to help Flan from the rubble of the explosion. Gray smoke filled her lungs and drifted across the parapets of Blakely Manor.

She picked her way around the hole the black powder had blasted in the roof and dragged her body—so worn and beaten she took little note of the cold and the wind that lashed at her—through the darkness toward the stone gargoyle.

"Uncle?" She collapsed against the low stone wall and reached for her uncle's hand. It was cold and still, swollen and bleeding where the ropes had cut into his wrists. "Uncle, please. Say something."

His large rough hand twitched under hers. One word drifted up to her through the darkness: "Flan?" It was so soft, she wasn't entirely certain she hadn't imagined it. Then another word, the anger behind it giving it more force: "Lucien?"

"He's gone, Uncle. He'll not bother us again." She leaned over the wall and gripped her uncle's arms. "We must get you home." She braced her feet against the base of the wall and pulled. She put all of her weight into it and pulled harder. She took a breath, gritted her teeth, and pulled yet harder.

So hard, she lost her grip and toppled over backward onto the pebbled roof.

"Ahhh!" She cried out in frustration and beat at the rough gravel with her fists. There had to be a way. She climbed to her feet once more and pushed the hair from her face.

"I will get you, Uncle. I will."

Flan closed her eyes and pushed her fingertips to her temples. Think. She needed to think.

"Flan." She felt Pascoe's icy touch on her arm.

She opened her eyes to find him sliding something from inside his soiled and tattered vest. It shimmered in the dim light, and she could see it was her bag, the silken evening bag she had lost.

He held it out to her. "I found it in the library. Will it help?"

Flan clutched the bag to her chest and closed her eyes. "Thank you."

The bag was unclasped, her spell ingredients spilling from its depths. As she plunged her hand into it, delving beneath the lining for her hazel wood wand, she sent out a silent plea: *Be there, be there, please be there.* At last her fingers, cut and bleeding and seared with pain, wrapped themselves around the smooth polished wood and the knobby silver cord. She thought she had never before felt anything so lovely.

She pulled out the wand and cast the bag aside.

"I will have you up in a twinkling, Uncle. Be patient but a few moments longer." She turned to Pascoe. "Once I lift him, will you be able to unbind his wrists?"

Pascoe nodded, and Flan turned back to her uncle. She squared herself before the stone gargoyle and aimed the wand at Anatole. She recited the levitation spell, her voice ringing out clear above the rushing wind.

The wand quivered. The air crackled. The very wind seemed to still.

And Uncle began to rise—slowly—first his robes, then his great white beard, then his head, his face drawn and pale, then shoulders, chest, arms, until his entire body hovered, inches above the gargoyle, skimming its worn stone surface. Flan lifted the wand, every muscle in her body tense—

—but she could not raise her uncle farther. She could not lift him above the gargoyle where she could hold him safe while Pascoe untethered the ropes. Her magic flowed from her mind, her heart, through her fingers and wand, and it simply was not strong enough.

As she let out another squeal of frustration, she saw Pascoe hold out his hands, palms up.

"I know some magic from before I was turned," Pascoe said. "I was never very powerful but perhaps in combination, my magic with yours . . . ?"

Flan closed her eyes. She could not do this. She could not combine her magic with the magic of a vampire.

But if she did not, she would never save her uncle. This time, this one time, she could not rely solely upon herself. She would have to accept his help.

She nodded, and Pascoe held his palms up. Together, combining their magic, they pulled Anatole up over the gargoyle, as far as the ropes, strained against his wrists, would allow. Flan threw herself across her uncle, clutching his arms, holding him fast, as Pascoe worked at the knots.

She hugged her uncle tight, pressing her ear to his chest, cheered by the steady beat of his heart.

"Hurry," she told Pascoe. "I don't know how much longer I can hold him."

"I'm trying." Pascoe dug at the thick ropes. "I know this knot. The ropes should come loose."

"Spelled." Anatole's voice was weak. Flan lifted her head to hear him better.

"The knot." Anatole licked his parched lips. "Lucien . . . spelled the knot."

Flan closed her eyes. She had never unspelled a rope, but if Pascoe could hold Uncle, she would find a way. She only hoped she could do it quickly.

"I will do it," said Anatole. "I know the kind of magic he used. I can reverse it."

"But, Uncle. The curse."

"I can do it."

Flan held tight. Pascoe, too, gripped Anatole's shoulders. The great wizard took a breath and began reciting the reversal spell, his voice growing strained, his face wrenched in pain. He closed his eyes. Sweat glistened on his lip.

"*ZEE-ast. VEE-* . . ." His incantation faltered. He licked his lips. "*Zee-ast* . . ."

He let out a groan and collapsed back against the gargoyle.

"Uncle." Flan gripped his hands. "Are you all right?"

Her uncle lay against the stone, his eyes closed, his lips pressed into a grim line. "I—I'm—give me but a moment, and we'll try again."

Flan pressed her cheek to his chest. She could not bear to see her uncle, the great wizard, in such pain, struggling so with his magic, felled by—what was it Lucien had said—a bit of wire and glass?

Flan stared at her uncle's pale face, glistening with sweat in the darkness. Horror dawned on her. The glasses. Her uncle's spectacles. All this time, all these weeks, the cursed object that had caused the tolling bells, that had hobbled Uncle's magic, had been right there on Uncle's nose.

Flan snatched the spectacles—the bit of wire and glass—from his face, threw them to the ground, and crushed them under her heel.

"Flan!" Her uncle's voice already sounded stronger. "How could you?"

"Try it now, Uncle."

Anatole frowned and closed his eyes. He began reciting the incantation once more. His face relaxed. His muscles loosened. His cheeks took on a glow. The ropes that bound him to the gargoyle quivered, snapped, then simply fell from his wrists.

Pascoe wrapped his arms around Anatole's shoulders, Flan held his chest, and together they hauled the great wizard over the gargoyle and onto the solid rooftop.

Flan sank to the pebbles beside him.

Anatole looked at her, a smile curling the corners of his

mouth. "Without my glasses, and in this gathering darkness, I can barely see you." He wrapped her in his arms and held his cheek to her head. "But my dear Flan, you are the most beautiful sight I could behold."

Flan breathed in the scent of him, listened to his strong heartbeat, hardly able to believe that he was back, that the danger was over.

"Now we must shuttle you home." She kissed him gently on the cheek. "A cup of tea and your own good bed will do much to restore your strength."

"Flan, dear, you need not mother me." Anatole struggled to rise from the pebbles. He braced a hand against the gargoyle. "But, I will allow, a hot cup of your fine chamomile tea with a stirring of honey would do me good."

Flan started to climb to her feet.

"Allow me."

She glanced up. Pascoe stood above her, hand outstretched. She grasped it, and he pulled her to her feet.

Flan brushed the gravel from her skirts and pushed a stray wisp of hair from her face.

"Was it painful?"

Flan looked up. "What?"

In the moonlight, she could see Pascoe smile. "You couldn't do it yourself. You needed to accept help—mine and your uncle's—and I just wanted to know, was it painful?"

Flan laughed. She held up her hands, bloodied and swollen, the sleeves of her gown torn and caked with ash. She took a step—gingerly, for she'd twisted her ankle and bloodied her knee in the blast.

231

She smiled. "No," she said. "It wasn't painful."

Flan cast a simple light spell, and with Anatole's arms around their shoulders for support, the three of them—Flan, Anatole, and Pascoe—made their way down the rough timber steps of the tower, through the great manor house, and out onto the freshly manicured lawns.

They rounded the courtyard to the spot where the vampire had fallen. Flan could barely bring herself to look up. But she knew she must. She had to assure herself that the danger was over, that she and her uncle and Wicker Street and all of the city would be safe.

She raised her eyes to the top of the courtyard wall—

—and saw nothing.

Lucien Kidd was gone.

Twenty-nine

Flan stared at the courtyard wall.

"Pascoe," she whispered.

He nodded. He had seen it too.

"Here." He changed direction suddenly, leading Flan and her uncle across the well-tended lawns. "Quickly. To the stream."

"But—" Flan glanced back at the manor house. "Gwen. Therese."

"Do not worry about them," Pascoe whispered. "Not now."

"But they must be here." Flan heard the panic in her own voice. "I haven't even searched for them. I can't simply leave them."

"And you won't. Just take your uncle and trust that they'll be safe."

They stumbled down the sloping lawn to the edge of the woods, and once again Flan thought she heard the rush of water. She'd heard it before, when she'd first arrived at Blakely Manor that evening—a mere two hours before, though it seemed an eternity.

As they pushed through the stand of willows and into the woods, she saw it. The water flowed freely once more, glinting in the faint moonlight as it rushed down the hillside, the current wide and strong.

Still bracing her uncle, Flan followed Pascoe down the slippery bank to a wide old oak, newly felled, the axe marks fresh at its base. It lay from bank to bank as a bridge across the surging water.

She frowned. Lucien Kidd had dammed the stream when he'd first come to Blakely Manor, which made much sense to her, for a vampire could not cross running water. By damming it, he could freely make his way into the city at night.

"Why would he undam it?" she said.

"Oh, but I wouldn't." The low silky voice rang out from the woods behind them.

Flan froze. He had survived. Somehow he had survived.

"Go." Pascoe pushed Flan and her uncle toward the felled oak. "Cross the water."

Flan stared at him. "You did this. You undammed the stream."

"When I found out you were invited to the manor, I suspected you would need an escape. Now go. Quickly. Lucien won't be able to follow."

"But neither will you," said Flan.

"Don't worry about me. Just take your uncle and go."

"I can't leave you." Flan scanned the woods, searching for the vampire. "Lucien is more powerful—"

"And injured."

"Which will only make him angrier."

"Which will only make him weaker. We don't have time for this, Flan. Your uncle doesn't have the strength."

"But what will become of you?" Flan felt tears pricking the corners of her eyes. Pascoe gripped her shoulders in his strong, slender hands, and as she looked up, the sweet, spicy scent of him whirled around her like a cloud. For a moment Flan simply stood there, held motionless once again by his pale gray eyes.

"We will meet again. I promise." He held her for a long moment, gazing into her eyes, his breath trembling in his chest. Or perhaps it was her breath that trembled. Her heart was beating so loud, she couldn't tell.

His head leaned in toward her. She felt her eyes close and—

"No," he said. He stepped back from her, holding her at arm's length, and she felt the very air collapse in her lungs.

"Someday," he whispered. "But not today. Not the way that I am now. But I will find a way and then I will find you." He still held her shoulders in his hands, and he turned her toward the stream. "Now go," he told her.

Flan swallowed her tears and nodded. She slipped the ash wood stake from her belt, and pressed it into his hand. "You may need this."

Pascoe took the stake, helped Flan steady her uncle onto the oak log, then turned back.

Midway across the stream, a chill black shadow fell over the woods, and a great flapping echoed through the trees. Flan looked back.

In the darkness, she could make out Pascoe high on the opposite bank, the wooden stake gripped at his side.

But as she watched, Lucien swooped from the trees. The shadow grew denser, as if he had sucked every bit of faint light from the air, until everything was black.

Flan caught her breath. She could see nothing. Not the far bank, not Pascoe, not even the water or log at her feet. And she could hear only the horrid flapping, an animal howl, and then a soft thud.

She held her uncle tight, and they crept across the log, one foot inching after the other. With each step, she feared her boot would slip from the bark of the oak tree, and she would tumble into the rushing water, dragging her uncle with her.

When finally her boot did slip from the wood, it sank into marshy soil.

Flan drew in a breath.

They had reached the far bank. She helped Uncle onto the shore and held his hand in hers.

Faint light began to seep through the trees once more. When she turned, she could see Lucien Kidd carrying Pascoe, limp and lifeless, from the woods.

Thirty

Lifeless.

She played the scene over and over in her mind, but no matter how she looked at it, which detail she examined, how hard she searched for some glimmer of hope, she could find no help for it. Pascoe had dangled from Lucien Kidd's arms, limp . . . and lifeless.

Flan bandaged Uncle's wrists and listened to his chest. His heart was strong, and she could detect no sign of lung fever or infection in his wounds. She settled him into bed with a cup of potent tea, stirred with a generous dollop of honey. She spelled the locks on the doors and windows, cast magical protections around the bookshop and upstairs rooms, and sank into her bed, Obsidian curled in her arms, her body bruised and weary, thinking—hoping—to fall into the deepest slumber of her life.

But sleep would not come. Her heart would not allow it. It would not loosen its hold on her mind.

She was home. Uncle was alive. It was what she had hoped for, what she had set out to do, the very reason she had dared venture into Blakely Manor.

But it was not enough. Her heart beat with relief and joy and gratitude—save for one hard kernel, deeply entrenched, that choked her with sorrow and regret.

Flan pulled her blankets to her chin and stared out into the moonless fog. She knew she had brought this all on. If only she hadn't tried those sleep spells, if only she hadn't stubbornly defied Uncle's wishes. Pascoe had paid dearly for her stubbornness, and she would carry that sorrow for the rest of her life.

Early the next morning, Uncle ambled into her bedchamber just as Flan was scraping the cedar chest from beneath her bed.

She sat back on the nubby rug. "You're looking chipper," she said.

And he was. He stood tall and wizardly, his face smoothed of the pain and worry that had racked his body these past days. His white hair cascaded to his shoulders, thick and gleaming, and high color glowed on his cheeks.

"I'm *feeling* chipper." He settled onto the edge of her bed and watched her. "The chest," he said after a moment.

Flan nodded. She held up the lace handkerchief. "I think it belongs with the other things."

"I believe it does."

Flan lifted the lid of the chest. If she had thought the handkerchief were only a gift from Lucien Kidd, she would have burned it the instant she arrived home, burned it till nothing was left save ash.

But it was more than that. She stroked the delicate lines of the lace. It was a connection to her parents. It was likely fashioned by her mother. She rubbed her finger over the handkerchief once more before placing it into the chest beside her baby gown. She was about to lower the lid when the scrap of crumbling brown paper caught her eye.

She picked it up. "It's Flannery Lace, you know."

"Yes."

Flan looked up. "My name, I mean. Not the handkerchief. All these years we thought the note said Lane, but it didn't. My name is truly Flannery Lace." She scrunched her nose.

"Your name is truly Katarina Maria Alexandra Blakely." Her uncle's voice was gentle.

Flan nodded. "Did you know? Have you known all along who I am?"

Anatole shrugged. "I suspected. It crossed my mind. I knew from your gown and your blanket that you must be of noble birth." He reached out and ran his knuckle along her cheek. "Raising you for fifteen years has shown me you also possess a noble soul." He tipped his head toward the handkerchief in the chest. "It all belongs to you, you know. Blakely Manor, the Blakely lands, the ancient Blakely title. It's rightfully yours."

"I suppose." Flan tucked the paper back into the chest and closed the lid. "It doesn't suit me. The name or the great hulk of a manor. I've gotten quite used to being Flan, the wizard's niece who lives above the bookshop." She smiled. "Can you picture me rattling around the great gaping halls of

Blakely Manor, calling myself Her Ladyship, the Viscountess Katarina Maria Alexandra Blakely?"

Her uncle laughed. Then his face grew more serious. He gazed down at her. "Truly, Flan, I can picture you doing anything you set out to do."

Flan blew out a breath. "Except magic. You were right, Uncle. My magic *was* a beacon for evil. I kept thinking magic could save things, but the more magic I used, the worse everything became. I should have listened to you."

"No, Flan. I was wrong. Magic is part of you, as much a part of you as your stubborn red hair." He brushed a stray curl from her cheek. "It runs stronger in you than in anyone I've ever known. I should never have forced you to ignore it. What I should have done—what I *will* do—is teach you how to use your natural-born gifts. Magic requires discipline, and you will be safer using powerful, disciplined magic than trying to deny magic you've yet learned to control."

Flan looked up at him. "Truly, Uncle?"

He nodded. "Truly." He climbed to his feet. "And who knows? Once you've learned all I can teach you, I may let you take over the magic business around here, so I can focus on what truly astounds me—science. We'll be a force to be reckoned with then, won't we? Combining your magic and my contraptions?"

Flan nodded. "We'll have to change the name of the shop." She traced the shape of a sign in the air. "Monsieur Anatole's Books, Wonders, Charms, and Inventions."

Anatole smiled. "I think that will do just fine."

As she pushed the cedar box back beneath her bed, a pounding sounded on the bookshop door.

Flan looked at her uncle. He shrugged. Flan scooped Obsidian into her arms and followed Anatole down the stairs.

They found Mr. Lindstrom, Gwen's father—perhaps the last person Flan would have expected—banging on the bookshop door. Mr. Lindstrom had not set foot in the shop, had not set foot on this end of Wicker Street, since the fire at the smithy.

Uncle unspelled the lock and pulled the door open.

"Anatole." Mr. Lindstrom pulled himself up to his full height. His twisted arm dangled at his side. "I've come to thank you." He swallowed, and his lip trembled ever so slightly. "Our Gwennie came home to us last evening just before supper, and we have only you to thank for it."

Flan felt her mouth drop open. "Gwen?"

Mr. Lindstrom nodded. "All she can remember is being kept in a cold, damp, dark place. Until last evening, about dusk, near as we can tell. She said a stranger led her from the place, set her free. When she finally pulled the blindfold from her eyes, she was alone on that wide boulevard what runs past the Blakely place."

Anatole narrowed his eyes. "A stranger."

"Aye. It's what she said. But don't take offense at it, Monsieur. She was blindfolded, see. All she could say was that he was tall and had a gentle way about him and that he smelled real nice."

His nose twitched in Anatole's direction, and Flan knew

he would be disappointed, for Uncle smelled of nothing but the liniment Flan had rubbed on his chest.

But Mr. Lindstom did not seem disappointed. "Sort of spicy, Gwennie told us." He cleared his throat. "Spicy and sweet."

Spicy and sweet.

Flan's mouth fell open.

Pascoe. It must have been him. Last evening, as Flan had been busy preparing for her visit to Blakely Manor, Pascoe had been even busier, rescuing Gwen, undamming the stream, felling a giant oak as a bridge over the water.

"What of Therese?" Flan said. "Has anything been seen of her?"

"Oh, yes." Mr. Lindstrom nodded. "Mrs. Childers said Therese came stumbling into the inn, all spooked and out of breath about the same time my Gwennie came home. She'd been freed. She couldn't say who'd rescued her any more than Gwennie could, but I know." He gave a curt nod. "I know it was you, Monsieur. For all the grief we've given you, you found it in your heart to help us anyway, and we thank you." He smiled then, and his smile nearly split his face in two. "It's a happy morning all around then."

Yes. Flan nodded. It certainly was—but for that one small hard kernel in her heart.

Life on Wicker Street soon returned to normal. The vampire had gone, and Blakely Manor, abandoned once more, returned to its wild and crumbling state. The townsfolk spent much time mulling over what could have happened to the new Lord Blakely.

"Couldn't take the pressure." The butcher gave a knowing nod. "That's what it was."

Mistress Dobbins shook her head. "Couldn't protect the people. That's what I think."

"Not made of the same stuff as the other Blakelys, that's for certain," said Mr. Jenks, and all of Wicker Street seemed to agree.

Flan could have told them that they were right. He was not made of the same stuff as the Blakelys. But she was not inclined to explain who he really was and why—and how—he had left. No use frightening them after he was gone.

Flan busied herself tending to the shop, putting the books in order, dusting the shelves, trying not to tangle her mind with thoughts of Pascoe Christopher. Her head told her she could not have done anything differently. She had Uncle to think of. She could not have left him on the riverbank to help Pascoe fight Lucien Kidd.

But the hard kernel in her heart dwelled on the ways she could have saved Pascoe, *should* have saved him, should have at least tried.

Instead, she had allowed Pascoe to sacrifice himself to save her, just as Xander sacrificed himself to save Katarina all those many years ago. Xander and Katarina. They were suddenly more than just names to her, more, even, than portraits hanging in a great hall. They were her parents. Her father had sacrificed himself to save her mother. And her mother had sacrificed much to save her baby—to save Flan. Was her mother still alive? Would she ever wish to see her daughter again?

She swallowed the lump in her throat. These thoughts tangled her mind if she allowed them. And so she spent her days dusting—truly dusting this time—and polishing the windows, and scrubbing the floors. The shop had never sparkled so.

Late one night Flan awoke suddenly. She sat up in bed and listened, for she was certain she'd heard a noise in the shop. She pulled her bed jacket close, scooped Obsidian in her arms, and made her way down the steps in her stocking feet, her lamp held high to light her way.

The bookshop was silent, the street beyond still, and Flan could see nothing out of place. She tried the door handle, and found it still latched and locked tight.

But as she turned to make her way back through the shop, her feet crunched through a scattering of leaves that were strewn before the doorway, as if they'd blown in from outside.

Odd. Flan frowned. She was certain she'd swept up before going upstairs for the night.

She set her lamp down to reach for the broom and noticed a book lying open on the work counter. Which was odder still.

It had been a slow day in the bookshop, and Flan had spent much of it tidying up. She knew she'd returned each and every book to its shelf. Had Uncle been unable to sleep? Had he come downstairs to read after she'd gone to bed?

She reached for the book and saw that this was a very familiar volume, a large, ancient tome, one of the books Pascoe had scoured through when he'd visited the shop. It was lying open, the page marked with a red thread.

Odd. Flan peered closer and saw that it had been opened to a passage about vampires returning to their human form.

Very odd indeed.

She turned the pages shut and heaved the book from the counter so that she could return it to its shelf.

But as she started across the shop, the ancient tome clutched tight to her chest, a sound floated toward her, faint and distant. It was music, a haunting melody, sad and sweet.

Her heart nearly leaped from her chest. There was only one person who could play that music—only one *vampire* who knew that melody.

For the music that soared above the empty city streets was from a lone violin, as if its soul had been set free to soar through the shadows and moonlight, yearning to reclaim what it had lost.

It was the nocturne.

About the Author

L.D. Harkrader is the author of twelve books for young readers, including three ghostwritten *Animorphs* titles. Her novel *Airball* (Roaring Brook Press, 2005) was a Junior Library Guild Selection, a New York Public Library Best Books for the Teen Age, a Bank Street College Best Book of the Year and it won the Friends of American Writers Juvenile Literary Award and the William Allen White Award. She lives in Kansas.

Don't wait until you're accepted into
wizardry school to begin your career
of adventure.

This go-to guide is filled with essential activities
for wannabe wizards who want to start

RIGHT NOW!
Ever wonder how to:

Make a monster-catching net?
Improvise a wand?
Capture a werewolf?
Escape a griffon?
Check a room for traps?

Find step-by-step answers to these questions and
many more in:

Young Wizards Handbook:

HOW TO TRAP A ZOMBIE, TRACK A VAMPIRE,
AND OTHER HANDS-ON ACTIVITIES
FOR MONSTER HUNTERS

by A.R. Rotruck

Books for
Young Readers

FORGOTTEN REALMS

R.A. SALVATORE & GENO

STONE OF TYMORA TRILOGY

Sail the treacherous seas of the Forgotten Realms® world with Maimun, a boy who couldn't imagine how unlucky it would be to be blessed by the goddess of luck. Chased by a demon, hunted by pirates, Maimun must discover the secret of the Stone of Tymora, before his luck runs out!

Book 1 THE STOWAWAY

Hardcover: 978-0-7869-5094-2
Paperback: 978-0-7869-5257-1

Book 2 THE SHADOWMASK

Hardcover: 978-0-7869-5147-5
Paperback:
available June 2010:
978-0-7869-5501-5

Book 3 THE SENTINELS

Hardcover:
available September 2010:
978-0-7869-5505-3
Paperback:
available in Fall 2011

"An exciting new tale from R.A. Salvatore, complete with his famously pulse-quickening action scenes and, of course, lots and lots of swordplay. If you're a fan of fantasy fiction, this book is not to be missed!"
—Kidzworld on *The Stowaway*

A DUNGEONS & DRAGONS NOVEL

Wizards
Books for
Young Readers

Want to Know Everything About Dragons?
Immerse yourself in these stories inspired by
The New York Times best-selling

A PRACTICAL GUIDE TO

DRAGONS

RED Dragon Codex	**BRONZE** Dragon Codex	**BLACK** Dragon Codex
978-0-7869-4925-0	978-0-7869-4930-4	978-0-7869-4972-4

BRASS Dragon Codex	**GREEN** Dragon Codex	**SILVER** Dragon Codex
978-0-7869-5108-6	978-0-7869-5145-1	978-0-7869-5253-3

GOLD
Dragon Codex

978-0-7869-5348-6

Experience the

power and magic

of dragonkind!